"Tanya wants what she can't have," Jake said

"And that's it?" Prudence gave a derisive hoot. "Her excuse was better. She said she'd been swimming."

"I think she had."

"She must keep her head high." He thought she was so stupid. "Look," she said, and the contempt came through, "I really don't care. So Tanya walks around your apartment wearing nothing but a smile and a pleased expression and you say you never knew anything about it. So what? Each to his own life-style."

Jake said evenly, "It would be asking a lot to ask you to trust me."

"Oh, it would." She nodded. "It would be asking too much. It's been nice knowing you, Jason Ballinger—but from now on, it's strictly business!"

Books by Jane Donnelly

HARLEQUIN ROMANCES

These books may be available at your local bookseller.

For a list of all titles currently available, send your name and address to:

Harlequin Reader Service
P.O. Box 52040, Phoenix, AZ 85072-2040
Canadian address: P.O. Box 2800, Postal Station A,
5170 Yonge St., Willowdale, Ont. M2N 5T5

Moon Lady

Jane Donnelly

Harlequin Books

TORONTO • NEW YORK • LONDON
AMSTERDAM • PARIS • SYDNEY • HAMBURG
STOCKHOLM • ATHENS • TOKYO • MILAN

Original hardcover edition published in 1984
by Mills & Boon Limited

ISBN 0-373-02649-8

Harlequin Romance first edition October 1984

CHAPTER ONE

THIS, mused Prudence Cormack, as she did every time, was surely one of the most exhilarating of sensations. Much more exciting than swimming—almost like making love, in its rise and fall of sheer delight. On this late autumn day, with the sun shining and the air cool and sharp, she was flying like a bird, the sails of her hang-glider billowing above her. She could hear the singing air in her sails, and below, farms and houses lay among the undulating fields like a child's model village scattered over a green carpet.

Prudence was an expert over this terrain. She knew how the air reacted here, where it became unstable, most of its tricks. In the three years since the lovely morning she made her first flight she had learned how to ride the wind so that on a good day she could stay up for hours, hovering, climbing, gliding, turning, and there was nothing like it for blowing away the blues.

A thermal of warmer air, rising from the ground up towards the clouds, lifted her glider higher. Now she could see over the hills to where the ancient monument of stones of pre-history looked like grey lozenges. Now her own home was matchbox size, the garden around it a mere patch. But it was a very important place, and she had the letters to prove that.

She smiled and slid the control bar to the right across her chest, swinging her body to the left so that the wing lowered on that side and the glider turned, and she took it into a glide, coasting downwards.

There were figures in the grounds of the big house; she had noticed them before. It might have been

5

interesting to know what they were saying, or even who they were, although as she came lower and the sun glinted on a man's coppery head she thought she recognised one of them. Well, she didn't exactly know him, but she knew plenty about him, and the day could be coming when she might reasonably expect to be meeting him.

He waved at her as she floated overhead. Her hang-glider sails were distinctive in wide blue-and-white stripes. Perhaps he was waving for the heck of it, or perhaps someone had told him, 'It's the Cormack girl.' If he did know who he was signalling he could skip the friendly gestures; they would get him nowhere. Last summer Prudence had been a guest when a hang-gliding club in the Midlands held a day of competitions and contests. In one event the flyers carried a water-filled balloon in their teeth and tried to drop it into a nearby pond. A splash meant a bullseye. It had been fun, and she thought now that she would enjoy dropping a water-filled balloon on Jason Ballinger. Or even something a good deal heavier.

The meadow beyond, at the foot of the hill, was an ideal landing site and she steadied her glider, but momentarily she had been rattled. Only for a second, not long enough to do any real damage. She pushed out the control bar, stalling the glider and bringing it to a halt, landing feet down, but briefly losing her balance.

She was up in a flash, quickly touching the nose of the glider to the ground before the wind could whip it up again, and as she began to slip out of her harness she heard him shout, 'Are you all right?'

He had arrived pretty darn quick. He must have started striding out when he saw she was landing, so he must have something to say to her, and this was the meeting she had been half expecting. 'Of course I'm all right,' she snapped. 'Which is more than we'll be when all your beastly helicopters start coming in!'

When she needed to be aggressive Prudence was, but she hadn't meant to go into attack when she met Jason Ballinger. She had meant to take a firm and very composed stand.

This was the first time she had spoken to him, although they had been neighbours since early spring. His name had come to this Wiltshire village before him when Radstone Manor, a rambling Victorian house, a hotel that had been running at no great profit in recent years, suddenly appeared in the local newspaper under 'Plans Before the Council', with a list of proposed conversions and improvements, for use as a conference centre.

Until then most of the locals hadn't realised that the Manor was on the market. It had been a family business for over fifty years, but the last generation had had other ideas, and other careers, and the hotel had become seedier as staff had been cut down, and for a long time there had been speculation about its future. Then suddenly, it was a fait accompli, and the ex-proprietors, Mr and Mrs Tilbury, couldn't get away fast enough to the luxury villa they were now able to buy in Denia.

Everyone wished them well. Times were tough and they were getting no younger, and it was a piece of good fortune that a property developer had dropped in for lunch one day when he was out looking for a place of this kind in this area.

The changing role of the old house had caused a flurry of local interest, with its prospect of jobs and trade. Ballinger and Merrick had their own construction team, but staff was going to be needed to run the conference centre, and interviews had already been held, and jobs promised. It was a talking point round here, and most of the excitement seemed centred on Jason Ballinger.

Quite early on Prudence had received an offer for her cottage, which had once been part of the stable block of the Manor. The stables had long been demolished, and the groom's cottage had changed hands several times before Prudence and her mother came to the village.

It had been for sale again then, structurally sound but badly needing all manner of small restorations, and it was exactly right for Prudence. She had worked on it and she loved it, and she had no intention of being moved. She had written back to the solicitors, who were acting for Ballinger and Merrick, explaining that.

It wasn't as though she was blocking off the drive or sitting in their backyard. She was tucked away, with a hawthorn hedge round her, and the Manor had acres enough, and she wasn't holding out for a better offer, she was simply not interested. But she got a better offer, and that was where her friends started to say, 'Well, I don't know, you could buy another house. It's a temptation, isn't it?'

'No,' she told them, 'I'm not tempted, and I'm not going.' She had nobody to please but herself now, unless she counted Percy. To date she had had three letters and a visit from an earnest middle-aged man who had arrived with positively their last offer and the explanation that where her cottage stood was a possible site for a block of garden rooms. 'You mean cabins?' she said, and he looked pained, 'Good heavens, no! We're not building a holiday camp here.'

'I don't care if you're drilling for oil,' Prudence had said. 'You can't do it on my land.' She had smiled as she spoke because her 'land' was such a tiny patch, but she was firm in her stand, and the man went away asking her to think it over. Which was pretty daft, as she had already had six months to do just that.

'Miss Cormack?' said Jason Ballinger.

'How did you guess?' said Prudence. He was not guessing, he had been told who she was; and she recognised him because she had seen his photograph in the press and he had been described to her by friends who had met him. Tall and lean, hawk-faced, with a slightly hooked nose and a long mouth, the skin tanned and the eyes hooded. He didn't look as if he laughed much, but when she spoke a corner of his mouth lifted, changing his expression into something mocking and wicked, and she felt a warning tingle in her blood. She was into an immediate clash of temperaments here, and she must watch her step.

'I'm Jake Ballinger,' he said.

'Of course you are.' Jason Ballinger, sometimes known as Jake.

His hair was dark red, and his skin was very brown as if he spent most of his time in the open air. There were lines across his forehead and round his eyes. It was a hard mouth, a hard face, and she could understand why he had created a stir when he'd strolled into the local pub. The girl who worked behind the bar had told Prudence, 'He looks like Clint Eastwood.' He didn't, except in height and breadth of shoulders, but Prudence could see what Tracey meant.

She took off her helmet, tossing back her hair. Heavy and waving, it fell around her shoulders, looking darker than it was because her skin was so pale. The wind had brought a faint flush to her cheeks.

'Are you going up again?' he asked.

'That's the idea.' Although actually she had been about to call it a day.

'Care to see around?' He looked towards the house,

which was opening for business in a couple of months, and which Prudence had been told was developing very impressively. In the early days she had walked over sometimes when no workmen were about, but she hadn't been near in recent weeks, although she supposed she was curious.

All the same it might be safer to say, 'No, thanks,' and trundle her glider back up the hill to rejoin her friends. There were two gliders in the sky, a group of folk on the hilltop, and by now those on the hilltop at least were watching Prudence talking to Jake Ballinger. They all knew about the offers for the cottage, and they all thought she was crazy not to sell as she was being offered more than the place was worth. Of course they couldn't understand her attitude, because there were things they didn't know, not even the friends who were closest to her.

If she went with Ballinger the question of selling would come up. That was why he had come over to talk to her.

And if she told the man at the top it might be the end of it; and she would like to see inside the house, and he was a challenge, just standing, looking at her, waiting for her answer.

She hardly seemed to hesitate. Really she had known as soon as he asked her that she was going with him. 'Bobby,' she called, 'would you——?' and a young man in hang-gliding gear detached himself from the group and came hurrying down the hill. 'Would you take this back for me?' she asked with a smile when he reached them. 'I'm going to look around the house.'

'Back home?' He had the look of an eager puppy, anxious to please.

'That would be a help,' she said.

'Leave it to me.'

'Bless you! I'll see you later.'

'Sure thing.' He said 'Hello' heartily to Jake Ballinger, who returned the greeting, and then set off up the hill carrying Prudence's glider.

'Is he yours?' asked Ballinger, as though Robert Bygrave *was* a puppy, instead of an intelligent young man who was making a good living as an estate agent. He could have been Prudence's, but she resented Ballinger's tone.

'No,' she said flatly.

'Just someone who comes when you whistle?'

'I don't whistle,' she said. 'I asked a friend to carry my glider back for me. I'd have taken charge of his for him, or of anyone else's. You don't *have* to be lovers.'

He laughed then, showing white teeth against the tan of his skin. 'Sorry, but he did look at you as though he'd have jumped off a cliff without his wings if you'd asked him to,' and she had to smile to herself. It was Bobby's spaniel-brown eyes, and maybe he would jump off a cliff at that.

'You're quite wrong,' she said crisply. 'The gardens are looking good. The grass is getting quite a different sheen on it viewed from up there.'

The lawns were tended now. The mowing lines ran straight, and freshly dug flowers beds showed rich earth. Prudence had watched that happening during the summer months, from her hang-glider. Down here the grass felt soft, when she stepped through a gap in the hedge from the field. The three men with whom Jake Ballinger had been talking were strolling towards the house, and Prudence and Ballinger followed across the lawns.

She suppressed an urge to start chattering. She wasn't nervous. High-powered business men didn't overawe her, and Jason Ballinger had no power over her, so there was no reason to be nervous. But something about him made her feel that if she touched him she would get a slight electric shock.

Let him talk, she thought. He came across to me, he invited me to look around. Let's hear what he has to say. Besides, if she did start chattering away she could end up sounding a fool.

She turned her head a little to look at him, striding along beside her, and at the same moment his head turned and their eyes met. They were both frowning slightly, and then he grinned and so did she. He certainly wasn't nervous of her, but he had been weighing her up and he seemed to like what he saw. She might have considered him attractive if circumstances had been different. Even in a couple of minutes she had found him—well, stimulating; but he was a tycoon and his stay here would be brief, and it didn't matter whether she liked him or not, she still wasn't selling him her little bit of land.

She had never been inside the Manor. She had known the family who ran the Manor Hotel, but this was the first time she had entered the house, and she could believe it had been transformed, because there was no sign now of hard times.

They went into a drawing room from a patio leading on to the lawns, and everything smelled clean and fresh and new. The reconstruction was finished, walls were being painted now. In here they were pale cream with gold leaf on the frieze and topping scrolls on two slim tall pillars of an archway. There would be a bar in the corner. It was set up in carved oak, waiting for stocks and customers, and of course the floors would be carpeted and there would be armchairs where the conference guests could sit to discuss the day's confabs and lectures.

'It's a big room,' she said. It was vast compared to her own home, where the walls closed in comfortingly

around her and there was hardly room to swing a cat.
'Don't say that in front of Percy!' she had joked when
somebody did. 'It'll take some heating,' she added,
inanely because of course his firm knew exactly what
their heating costs were going to be, and he shrugged.

'There'll be a lot of hot air.'

He meant talk, all those interminable business
discussions. Prudence could almost hear the hum of
voices, and through an open door men were talking, the
ones who had strolled into the house ahead of them.

The hall was a good size too, with a curving
staircase leading up to a gallery. The walls were still
plaster-white here, but the ornate fireplace was
probably the original. In Victorian black marble, it
would be rather splendid when it was cleaned and
polished. As they were opening at the beginning of the
year there would probably be logs burning and big
fires built up. Pictures on the walls, she supposed, and
she looked at the empty space over the fireplace and
asked, 'What will be up there? A portrait of you?'

'I don't go in for portraits,' he said. 'Do you swim?'

'Well, yes.' She had heard there was an indoor pool,
and saunas and squash courts, and now she followed
him down a corridor that opened into the sports area.
All the pool, tiled in aquamarine with the round tub of
a jacuzzi beside it, lacked was water. 'Nothing but the
best,' she commented.

'That's always been my motto.'

'Lucky you.' He had the confidence of a man who
considered the best his due, and from what she had
heard his ventures never failed.

'You don't approve?' She must have sounded ironic.
They were walking towards the far end of the pool,
and she looked down into the shining tiles and said,

'Why not go for the best if you're prepared to pay
for it?'

'I am. So long as I get value.'

She still looked down. The water would be deep enough for diving here. She could imagine the shimmer of it and how it would feel against the skin, and she shivered as though she had dived in and found it cold. No one would cheat Jason Ballinger, although he was probably not above sharp practice himself in clinching a deal or manipulating a situation. Men like him kept up their lifestyle, but they could cause havoc and heartbreak in other people's lives.

'Steady!' he said suddenly, as his fingers closed on her elbow. She wouldn't have overbalanced, although she was standing on the edge and her shoes were thick-soled sneakers, but he pulled her back. 'Wait till the water's in,' he said. He didn't release her right away. His hold was light, guiding her along, but she was very conscious of it, although through a heavy denim jacket she shouldn't have felt a thing.

She started to talk, easing away from his touch, admiring the décor and the layout. This was going to be a stylish place, and she said so, although she didn't gush. In fact her approval was a little grudging because she would rather the old house had stayed as it was. Showing a healthier profit, of course, but she had liked its faded gentility, overgrown gardens, the guests coming and going quietly.

Jason Ballinger often arrived in a helicopter, and so would others, and there would be streams of powerful cars zooming through the village driven by sharp-eyed characters whose credo was success at any price. Now she had met him Prudence admitted that he had charm, but she was wary of his kind.

She said the right things as he showed her round. She was getting a conducted tour, which was neighbourly of him. 'My goodness,' she murmured at intervals, then she followed him through a door at the end of a corridor into a smallish room that was a genuine surprise. 'Oh, I like this!' she cried.

It was the only furnished room. There were brown fur rugs on this polished floor, squashy tan leather armchairs, and a matching sofa that could be a bed. There were papers on a flat-topped desk, a phone on the windowsill in the circular alcove of a tower. It looked a combination of clutter and comfort, and she went over to the window. She could see the spinney and the hedge around her cottage from here, and the rooftop and the three dormer windows. 'There's something about towers, isn't there?' she mused. 'I think this could be my favourite room. The others are all quite splendid, but I rather like the shape of this one.'

'I'm using it at the moment,' he said. 'If you changed your mind about selling maybe I could give you a lease here. Including this room if you liked.'

A flat in this house was an attractive offer and that was probably why he was showing her round, but she said lightly, 'Thanks, but no thanks.'

'What is your price?' He had come close behind her. If she swayed back she would be against him, and she leaned forward slightly, making a show of looking to left and right, telling him, 'My house isn't for sale. What do I have to do to make you believe me? Why are you so set on getting your hands on my little cabbage patch anyway? I'm not bothering you.'

'I wouldn't say that.' His tone made her turn, and smile because he was smiling in frankly sexual appraisal, and it was a compliment no matter what his motives were. She could have said the same herself. He was a disturbing man and she was beginning to enjoy this. 'A drink?' he offered, and opened a cupboard on glasses and bottles.

'Thank you.' Prudence took a dry sherry. He

poured whisky into a glass and she sat down in one of the squashy chairs and asked, 'Do you move around much?'

'All the time.'

That was what she thought. 'Then you won't understand why I don't want to dig up my roots,' she said.

'Fair enough, we'll forget it.' She was not sure that he would, but she said, 'I already have.'

'Have you lived here long?' She supposed she had sounded as though generations of her family had been born and bred in Stable Cottage.

'Since I was seventeen,' she said.

'Just a couple of years.'

'And the rest.' She was twenty-four now.

'What do you do for a living?'

He might be making polite conversation. He sat still and relaxed watching her over the glass he held, but she knew he was a powerhouse of energy with a mind like a steel trap, and she thought, He knows how long I have lived here and he knows how I earn my living. 'You know what I do,' she said.

An eyebrow raised. 'Famous, are you?'

'No, but you've been trying to buy me up ever since you bought this house, and I'm sure you know how long I've had Stable Cottage. Anyone in the village would have told you, and that I've got a little shop in Bath.'

He smiled. 'Nobody said a word against you. Well,' he went on smiling, 'nothing I could blackmail you with.'

A cold finger ran down her spine, and she felt its icy trail. 'I suppose I could try persuasion,' he said, and his voice was drawling, teasing, and she made her own lips lift and shook her head.

'It would be a pity to waste your time. I'm sure it must be very valuable.'

'I can be very persuasive.'

'One of the best, I'm sure.' They were fooling, but of course he was an expert in persuasion, whether his object was money or sex. 'Very persuasive,' she said gaily, 'but not over-modest.' She put her glass on a small table beside her chair and then clasped her hands together because the shiver in her spine couldn't be held down. Briefly she had the shakes.

'Are you cold?' It wasn't all that warm in here, there was no central heating on, and he switched on a blow-heater, although she protested, 'I'm fine, really, somebody must have walked over my grave,' and almost shivered again hearing herself say that.

After that it was very pleasant. They talked easily. Jake Ballinger told her his plans for the place, which she knew anyway, everyone did, but she had to agree that if he hadn't bought the old house its years would have been numbered. She said, 'I'm sure it will be a success, but I don't want my cottage being swallowed up.'

'I wouldn't even try.' There was no way he could turn her out if she didn't want to sell, and she was sure he wasted no time on lost causes. 'I'll drink to that,' she said, and lifted her glass to her lips but she couldn't know his thoughts, what he was toasting.

'Who would that be?' he asked. There was still one hang-glider, framed in the window, drifting slowly across the sky. Prudence recognised the sails and told him, 'He's a farmer—Joe Howard from Upper Meon.' She looked at Jake Ballinger, from under her long dark lashes. 'Are you a sporting man?'

'Not enough to get me up there without an engine. I like power under my belt.'

'We can't all afford power. Anyway, the wind lifts you. You ride it. It's fantastic, almost like being a bird. Men flew with wings before machines, you know.'

'Sure,' he said. 'Icarus. Only he got too near the sun and his wax melted.'

'Well, I never get too near the sun and I'm not a melting lady.'

She could say that with truth, laughing and pushing back her dark heavy hair. But by now it was getting warmer in here and she unzipped her jacket. She wore a smooth-fitting sweater beneath it, and a silver moon pendant on a thin chain. She saw him looking at that. 'Your design?' he asked.

'My trademark—the moon.' She designed and made jewellery, working always in silver or silvery alloys, and her signature was a crescent moon. Her prices were reasonable and she sold well enough, in a shop she shared with a friend, and through others in the district.

'May I?' He got up from his chair, crossed to hers and lifted the pendant to examine it, and she said, 'It's nothing special. It's just a moon with a moonstone that I like to wear myself. I do prettier things. If you're considering opening a boutique here, local gifts to take back to folk at home, you ought to give my jewellery a chance. You can't get much more local than me. I'm your next-door neighbour.'

It was an idea, and she was always on the lookout for markets. But she was talking fast because he was too close for comfort, his face just above hers, holding her by the thin chain. She could feel his breath on her lips and see dark flecks in his grey eyes. She didn't want to break the chain by jerking back, but she didn't like this situation at all.

'I'll think about it,' he said, and the phone rang. Saved by the bell, she thought, and nearly said it, which would have been crazy, and embarrassing, because what did she imagine she was being saved from? Jake Ballinger was hardly about to molest her.

'Ballinger,' he said briskly, and then, 'Oh, hello,' in a different tone. He was talking to a woman whom he would be meeting this evening. The conversation was brief, but that was how Prudence interpreted it, and it reminded her that she should be on her way because Bobby was coming to supper. She stood, and when Jake put down the phone she said, 'I must be going. Thanks for showing me round.'

'A pleasure.'

There seemed to be no one else in the building now. As they came down the big echoing staircase Prudence could hear no voices, and she felt a sense of emptiness. She left by the front door, saying goodbye, and heard it close as she walked away. She presumed he would go back now to the room that was habitable, because that was home for the time being. By the end of the year home for him would be somewhere else, because Jake Ballinger moved around all the time.

He seemed to thrive on it. His life obviously suited him. She wondered who the woman was with whom he was spending the evening and if that meant the night, and thought it was unlikely she was local because that kind of gossip would soon have got around.

Prudence's hang-glider, neatly packaged, lay across her garage door. Bobby had brought it, possibly expecting to find her here; when she looked at her wrist watch she realised that her tour of the house had taken over two hours. Bobby would be back. She had a quiche cooked and a bottle of white wine in the fridge, because she owed him for a couple of dinners and Prudence liked to balance her books.

More than one man had accused her of being too independent. It wasn't often meant as a compliment, although it was usually said affectionately. She never lacked admirers because she was a striking-looking girl, tall and slim, with her cloud of dark hair, her translucent skin and silver-grey eyes. She was fun to be with, she had a quick, sometimes crazy, sense of humour, and Robert Bygrave thought she was the kind of woman he wouldn't mind spending the rest of his life with.

Since her mother died Prudence had lived alone, but it never occurred to anyone that she might be lonely. She had so many friends, and always a man to call on. All this summer the man had been Bobby. Percy was getting used to him, although Percy welcomed nobody but Prudence.

He was a handsome marmalade cat, striped like a tiger, sleek and well fed as any pampered pet, but still with the instincts of the scrawny wild kitten that she had lured into her home with patience and perseverance over four years before.

He was waiting for her now. He got out of the tub-chair beside the stove as she walked into the living room and padded to meet her and she stooped to stroke him. Her touch was very gentle. She was the only one who petted Percy with impunity. His claws could draw blood if anyone else was rash enough to try, but for Prudence he purred and then went back to his chair, settling down with a sigh of satisfaction. So far as the cat was concerned nobody else was needed in here. When Bobby came he would probably stalk off into the kitchen, through the cat-flap and out into the night.

Prudence unlaced her sneakers, kicked them off and got out of her hang-gliding suit. It wasn't flattering wear. It was comfortable and right and protective for the sport, but she could have had a thick waist and legs like young tree trunks under that lot and nobody would have known. She pulled off her sweater and stood, in tights, pants and bra, looking at her long slender legs and wondering again about the woman on the phone just now. I'll bet my figure's as good, she thought. Unless she's a model or something spectacular I might compare all right.

Then she grimaced at herself, because she wasn't competing for Jake Ballinger. Probably she wouldn't even see him again, so he would never know that she had rather super legs. 'Pity, though,' she said to Percy, who was fast asleep, and she put the quiche in the oven to warm, then went upstairs to make herself presentable for Bobby.

It wasn't hard. Bobby always thought she was attractive. She could always rely on him to say, 'You look lovely,' but tonight she took extra care.

The dress she had planned to wear was lying on her bed, dusky pink in light soft wool, worn with black patent pumps and a wide black patent belt. Prudence was quick and competent with her make-up. She knew exactly how to use eye-shadow and mascara so that her eyes sparkled and her long lashes were emphasised. She knew the shape of her face after twenty-four years. Putting on cosmetics was as easy as combing her hair. But tonight she sat at the dressing table, studying her reflection as though it was a stranger's, applying colours slowly.

It was not a bad face at all. She was not a raving beauty, but by candlelight she might pass for one. She had been told she was unforgettable—sometimes by men who had managed to forget her, or at least replace her when she sent them on their way. I wonder what kind of impression I made just now, she thought, I wonder if I'll see him again.

She wouldn't go looking. She wasn't that interested. But if he should phone her, or come calling she wouldn't be displeased. Within limits she wouldn't mind seeing more of Jake Ballinger.

When Bobby knocked on her door she was still sitting at her dressing table holding her lipstick, and she applied it quickly and hurried downstairs to let him in. He was in cords and cream Aran polo-neck now, and he said, 'You look good enough to eat,' and reached to hug her against the rough wool of his sweater. 'Did you see round?' he asked, following her down the little hall into her living room.

'Yes. It's going to be everything they say.'

Robert Bygrave knew that. He was in the property business himself, as junior partner in a local firm, and he was interested in what the big league boys were doing when they moved into his area.

Percy got off his chair and walked past them, making for the cat-flap in the kitchen door, pausing briefly to spit at Bobby, who said, 'Your cat's manners get no better.'

'Maybe a hair from your jumper got up his nose,' Prudence teased, and he grinned.

'Everybody gets up his nose, I never knew such a bad-tempered brute.'

'I think he's lovely,' she said.

'Can't think why,' said Bobby. 'You don't have a thing in common.'

She left him turning the pages of a Sunday colour supplement while she scurried around in the kitchen. She had expected to have all this done before he came, but she had been later back than she'd expected, and even when she was home time had somehow drifted by. The quiche was fine, and she cut hunks of wholemeal bread, and tossed a salad, putting everything on a tray and carrying it on to the big old round mahogany table in the living room. 'Get glasses out of the cupboard for me, would you?' she asked. 'And the wine's in the fridge.'

As they sat down to eat Bobby enquired, 'What did

he have to say? Why did he come over to invite you to go round the house?'

'To talk about the cottage, of course.'

'Well?' Bobby prompted, and she finished chewing a mouthful of quiche. Bobby thought she should take the money. He couldn't have got her a price like that on the open market, and although she had made this place very comfortable she could do that just as easily with somewhere else. This wasn't a listed building. It was a Victorian workman's cottage, poky and probably with rising damp. 'I could show you half a dozen places tomorrow that would leave you with a few thousand quid to play with,' he said.

'He offered me a lease in the Manor. He said I could have one of the tower rooms.' She smiled, 'And the use of the swimming pool, I suppose, with all those business conference bods splashing around.'

Boddy wasn't so sure about that. 'What did you say?' he asked, and she shook her head.

'I don't want to move, that's what I said.'

'Well, you know your own business.' He didn't much fancy her moving into the conference centre, but several times he had offered his professional opinion and he was always a little hurt that she never even stopped to consider. He supposed it was because this was a link with her mother, and they had been very close. Prudence had no other relations and this must be like a family home to her.

'What did you think of him?' asked Bobby, and she sipped her wine and said lightly, 'I thought he looked like his photographs. He's obviously the boss and he's obviously as hard as nails.'

She wondered if his face would soften tonight looking at the woman who had phoned him. He was so vividly in her mind that she could almost imagine he was sitting in that chair opposite, not Bobby.

'Did you like him?' Bobby was asking, and she shrugged.

'Why not? There was nothing to dislike. He showed me round and asked me what price I'd consider for the cottage, but when I said I didn't want to sell he didn't push it.'

She wouldn't like to be fighting him, he would be a ruthless enemy, and Bobby reached across to stroke her cheek, relieved that Jason Ballinger seemed to have made no particular impression on her. For the rest of the meal they never mentioned Ballinger's name again, but Prudence couldn't get him out of her mind.

Bobby's whole attention was on Prudence. He always found it hard to keep his eyes and his hands off her. Her silky hair, the smooth texture of her skin, and her full sensuous mouth captivated him. In the last seven years others had fallen for her, some of them friends of his, but she never seemed interested in a real commitment. She liked to keep her relationships light, and Bobby was never quite sure that one of these days she might not decide that he and she were spending too much time together.

If she ever said that it wouldn't mean she was angling for marriage. It would mean that she would be busy when he phoned and there would be an easing off, a stepping back. If he wanted to stay friends he would have a friend in her, but the closeness would be over. Some of Prudence's exes had been indignant when they got the brush-off, demanding to be told what the hell they had done. There had been some noisy scenes before they marched off in a huff of macho pride and looked around for somebody else.

Robert Bygrave knew all this. He thought it was ridiculous that a girl as sensuous as Prudence should be called frigid, which was one of the accusations levelled against her. He preferred to believe she hadn't met the right man until he came along.

Prudence had expected to pass this evening undisturbed. Just the two of them having a quiet meal, then curled up together in her big old chesterfield in front of the stove in the living room. Maybe watching television. Maybe not. But comfortable, because Bobby was a nice man who thought a lot of her, and no danger.

She put coffee down in front of them and poured brandies, they sat with her feet tucked beneath her, her head on his shoulder, his arm around her, and the TV turned on. And he told her he loved her and kissed her tenderly, and she kissed him back. Then she poured more coffee and for most of the time they watched the film. The rest of the time they talked, because Prudence mentioned that Sally had phoned just before Bobby came and asked if she could look in this evening. She had something very important she wanted to discuss that couldn't wait till morning.

'I couldn't very well say no,' Prudence explained.

Sally Loring worked with Prudence, and her life moved from one trauma to the next, so Bobby was not surprised to hear that she had problem she was bringing to Prudence. He did wish, though, that Prudence had insisted it would *have* to wait till tomorrow, because now there was a risk of Sally battering on the door at any minute. After Prudence had kissed him she had drawn back, and as his arms had tightened she had said, very quickly, 'I'm sorry, but there's company coming.'

'Company?' Bobby had howled. 'You don't mean Ballinger?'

'Of course I don't—er—Sally.' And she explained about the phone call and poured a coffee, and after that he had to settle for kisses and a large measure of self-control.

'She'll never turn up now,' he said hopefully around ten o'clock.

'Don't you believe it,' said Prudence. 'I've had her round here at midnight. When she found out that traveller had a wife and four children she woke me up to ask me if I thought his wife would divorce him.'

Bobby grinned, 'What did you say?'

'I said she probably had,' said Prudence. 'I wonder where my cat's got to.' She went to the back door, and cold air blew in, and it dawned on Bobby that he was about to overstay his welcome.

She called, but there was no sign of Percy, and Bobby said, 'I'll be going, then, shall I?'

'Well,' said Prudence, 'I do have an early appointment.'

He kissed her again, and she stood at her front door and waved goodbye as his car drove away. He had believed her about Sally. She felt rather ashamed that she had resorted to such a silly trick, but she had been caught off balance, it had been upsetting, and now she must pull herself together.

It was a dark night, no moonlight and no stars, just one lamp burning down the village street now that the rear lights of Bobby's car had vanished. From the back of the house she could see a glow in that turret window and wondered if Jake Ballinger was entertaining his lady friend up there.

She left the kitchen door open, so that some light filtered out, and began to whistle the cat, walking down the garden path to where the hedge backed on to the spinney and calling, 'The coast's clear, love, you can come in now.'

She couldn't see him, but on the other side of the hedge she heard him laugh and then he said,

'Now there's an offer!'

Prudence nearly jumped out of her skin. 'Jake?' she yelped.

'Who else?'

It could have been anybody else, but she had known him by his laugh before he spoke. 'Actually,' she told him, 'it was Percy I was whistling.'

'I thought you didn't whistle.'

'Percy's different. I do a lot of things for Percy I wouldn't be doing for anybody else.'

She could see Jake as a dark shadow through the gap in the hedge. If there had been no hedge she could have reached out and touched him, and she wondered if he was alone or if he had been walking in the gardens with a friend who was just behind him, out of sight. 'Does he hang around much out here?' Jake enquired.

'Yes. Would you have seen him?'

'Describe him.'

'Oh, he's a tiger.' She whistled again. 'But he likes the house to himself, and up to now I've had company.'

A pale sinuous shape came out of the copse, and darted through the hedge down the garden path into the house. 'Bobby went early,' said Jake . . . 'See you later,' she had said when Bobby went off with her glider. His date hadn't gone on into the small hours either, although it wasn't that early.

'I've a busy day tomorrow,' she explained.

'I showed you round my place, how about showing me round yours?' That wouldn't take long, but it would be taking too much of a risk.

'Not tonight,' she said.

'Another time?'

'Maybe.' There were thorns on the hawthorn hedge. She saw him through the thorns and said, 'Goodnight.'

'And to you.'

He must have been out here, in the gardens, and heard her calling the first time and strolled over. He had come when she whistled, and she locked the kitchen door after her, and sat down on the hearthrug in front of the stove stroking Percy. 'You weren't the only tiger out there tonight,' she told him.

She had no illusions abut Jake Ballinger. He was the killer kind, she knew that. She would watch he never got his claws into her. But that little exchange through the hawthorn hedge had left her smiling and exhilarated. When she kissed Bobby tonight she had wondered how it would be to kiss Jake and feel his arms around her, and lust and longing had stirred in her, but not for Bobby. She had lied about Sally coming because that was easier, and less hurtful, than saying, 'Please go. Or if you must stay a while please don't try to make love to me, because for some crazy reason I can't stop thinking about another man.'

CHAPTER TWO

PRUDENCE woke feeling refreshed and ready for the day, and sat up stretching and smiling. Maybe she had been dreaming, because it was as though something fantastic had been happening, leaving her with an aftermath of tingling elation. And perhaps it was as well she couldn't remember, because she was fairly certain who had been in her dreams with her.

There was a glitter of frost on the trees of the spinney when she went to the window to look across at the big house, reminding her that she should be ordering some logs. Her woodpile was low and winter was coming.

'Good morning,' she said, 'and I don't suppose you dreamed of me.' Then she hurried into the bathroom and into the whirl of her early morning routine: washing, dressing, gulping a cup of coffee and spooning down muesli, while she darted about, feeding the cat and doing the chores and listening to the radio for time checks.

She never sat down to breakfast. She never had since her mother died. They used to breakfast together, otherwise Priscilla Cormack might not have bothered with food all day. She always had an evening meal ready when Prudence came home from work, but Prudence had to coax her to eat herself.

A couple of letters plopped through the letterbox on to the hall floor and Prudence picked them up, giving the envelopes a quick glance. They were both addressed to Miss Prudence Cormack. Nobody else lived here, so of course that was the name on the envelope, and she scanned the contents. Neither needed immediate attention, and she put them in a silver toast-rack that she used for letters on the sideboard.

She aimed to be at work for nine o'clock, which meant leaving home around half past eight, but this morning she was still here at almost a quarter to nine, and she was turning the key in the front door when she heard the phone ring. She had the door open again and was inside the hall before it burred a third time, pouncing on it so that her 'Hello' was a little breathless.

'I thought you might have gone,' said a girl's voice. 'About tonight—could you bring along another bottle of white rum, I'm not too thrilled about the punch.'

'Yes, of course!' Prudence smiled ruefully as she replaced the receiver, although that had been one of her best friends, because she had thought it could be Jake. She was sure he would be in touch, he might have picked up the phone in his room and called to say good morning. She didn't usually hang around waiting for phone calls, and she told herself now that she hadn't been waiting, it was just that she was a little later than usual this morning.

Anyhow, there was nothing serious about this. Anything that developed between herself and Jason Ballinger would be brief and amusing. She grinned at the cat, who was sitting on the grass beside the garage door, waiting for her car to leave as it did every weekday. 'Anyhow,' she said, 'you'd have thought he might have said good morning, wouldn't you; after the way he was carrying on last night in my dreams?'

She would have to put her foot down now to make up for lost time, and she hoped the road would be clear. Her car was her pride and joy, a white B.M.W. that she had bought second-hand six months before. It had almost cleared her bank account, but it had been a good buy. She was a skilful driver and her car gave her the same thrill as her hang-glider, a feeling of being in control, going where she liked, driving fast, flying high.

The first week she had the car she had sat at traffic lights, windows and sun roof open, her shining hair tumbling over her shoulders, wearing an ice-blue sleeveless silk dress; and a lorry driver, revving up beside her, had leaned out of his cab and called down, 'Hello, darlin', did Daddy buy you that?'

'Of course,' she had said, flashing him a brilliant smile. Afterwards she had started laughing, and had to draw up by the side of the road and sit quietly for a moment or two, biting her lip, because the laughter was hurting.

The road from the village to the town took her past the stones of Eyesford. They were scattered all around this area, and must once have been a vast complex bigger and probably older than Stonehenge. Now, even from the air, the design was lost, but there were broken rows of them across fields, clusters here and there. Two, worn and weatherbeaten until they looked like something monstrous and crouching, were at the roadside.

Prudence liked them, especially the roadside pair. They could look weird in the fog, or if you didn't expect to see them. Cars were always skidding along this stretch, but she felt they were friendly. Permanent, anyway. Roots didn't go much deeper than those stone monoliths reaching down into the earth.

The party tonight was being held at one of the houses she passed, up on a hill, near one of the better preserved circles. The last day of October, Hallowe'en—just the time and the place for a party, and the Howards were great party-givers. Prudence had met Jean Howard when she was training in jewellery production at the County Polytechnic, and Jean was doing a secretarial course, and they had been friends ever since. Jean was married now, expecting her first baby, and Prudence was helping with tonight's buffet.

She would know almost all the guests and she was looking forward to it, although she hoped that Bobby wouldn't monopolise her. She sighed, changing down a gear rounding a corner, and her thoughts switched abruptly to Jake, as though he shoved Bobby away. That didn't take much doing, Bobby had never obsessed her when he wasn't around. She *had* thought about him, of course, but Jake Ballinger seemed to be *here*.

Nothing very much had been done or said during the time she had spent with him yesterday, but he could hardly have left a deeper impression if they had passed the entire two hours in passionate lovemaking or he had threatened to kill her. Even when she slept her dreams had been filled with him, she could remember that much. Right now she could almost feel his breath on her lips again, and she jerked back in her seat and an oncoming car's hooter blared as she veered into its path. She wrenched her wheel round in the nick of time, passing the motorist's furious face mouthing obscenities.

He must have thought she was drunk, or trying to commit suicide. It was the unforgivable idiocy, thinking of something else while you were driving. After that Prudence kept her eyes on the road, but she was angry with herself. A head-on collision had been averted by a split second because she was mooning about a man she hardly knew.

She parked her car in her space behind the shop and said hello to a couple of her trading neighbours who were getting out of their van at the same time. They ran a D.I.Y. paint-and-wallpaper shop, and the woman paused to take another look at Prudence and ask, 'Are you all right? You look a bit off colour.'

'I nearly had an accident just now.' She was probably even paler than usual, and the woman said indignantly, 'There are some fools on the roads. Half of them shouldn't be allowed behind a wheel!' She and her husband took it for granted that Prudence was blameless and sympathised with her all the way to her front door. She could hardly confess that she was the fool, and she went into the shop smiling because she didn't want to have to explain to Sally, or anybody else, why she looked shaky.

While Prudence was a student she had worked here, holidays and weekends, helping the two elderly spinsters who ran it as a wool shop. They had put her early pieces on display, she had made her first sales from here. They were fond of Prudence and her dear mother and when they retired Prudence, who was then nineteen, had taken over the lease. She had turned a cellar into a studio workroom where she designed and made her jewellery and upgraded the wool shop into a high-fashion knitwear boutique. For the last three years Sally Loring, who knitted beautifully, had been producing most of the handmade sweaters and jackets and suits.

It was a classy little shop. Sally lived in the flatlet above, and when Prudence left here at midday on Saturday so had Adrian Foster, Sally's boy-friend.

It wouldn't have mattered this morning if Prudence had been shaking like a leaf, because Sally's eyes were puffy pink slits and it was Prudence who asked 'What's up?' her heart sinking because she knew. Sally was usually a very pretty grl, with limpid eyes and dimples, but the dimples weren't in evidence this morning.

'Adrian's gone,' she said mournfully. 'We had the most awful row. He didn't come home until this morning, and then—oh, it was *awful*!'

'Oh dear,' said Prudence. 'How about a cup of tea?'

She couldn't see that it was going to be much of a loss if Adrian Foster stayed away, because recently he hadn't been making Sally very happy. He was a flashily good-looking young man with a lot of blond wavy hair, who never passed a mirror or a shop window without giving himself an admiring glance. Prudence considered he had too high an opinion of himself, he certainly had a roving eye, but Sally always threw herself, heart and soul, into her love affairs. Her love could do no wrong, and she resolutely refused to recognise the danger signals.

Adrian had been cooling off for weeks. Sally put his neglect down to overwork, which Prudence didn't believe for a minute. Several of Sally's friends had reported seeing him with other girls, the crash was coming, although Sally went on pretending. Only last week she had finished an exquisite lacy suit, in a pale lilac that would have looked lovely on a bride, and said as they arranged it on display, 'I think I'll do this pattern for my wedding.'

Prudence had been kneeling in the window, spreading the skirt, her mouth full of pins. She nearly swallowed a pin, gasping, 'Your *wedding*?' and Sally said,

'Well, we'll be getting married some time. I've been wondering, do you think I should start a baby? Do you think that might——'

At that Prudence spat out all the pins and shrieked, 'For pity's sake, *no!*'

'He's so gorgeous, though, isn't he?' Sally had sighed. 'Like a Greek god. I'm so lucky to have him.' She didn't have him, he was going to walk out on her, but she wouldn't face that until it happened, and Prudence had sighed too, and then finished pinning up the suit.

The suit was still in the window. Later today Prudence would take it out, although it had brought in several women to buy the wool and the pattern, and would eventually have found one who could afford to buy the suit. Poor Sally didn't need reminding of wedding outfits.

'I'll make the tea,' said Prudence, and ran up the narrow creaking stairs. The flatlet was usually in immaculate order, Sally kept it neat as a pin, but this morning drawers were open and the wardrobe gaped wide. After the 'awful' row Adrian must have packed at speed. All his clothes seemed to have gone. While she waited for the kettle to boil Prudence walked round, shutting drawers. He could have done that at least, she felt, left the place as he'd found it.

A photograph in a silver frame, grinning boyishly, caught her eye. She had seen it before, of course, but now she stood looking at it until the kettle clicked off.

'Like a Greek god,' Sally had said. More like a tailor's dummy, thought Prudence. I've seen faces like that in many a window. Good riddance, she thought, and she took it off the windowsill and dropped it into a drawer. Then she made tea in two royal blue enamel mugs and carried them downstairs.

Sally was sitting in the little storeroom-cum-office at the back of the shop, knitting away. Her fingers seemed to be working independently of the rest of her. She didn't look down at the clicking needles when Prudence put a mug on the old leather-topped desk in front of her. 'I just came down,' she said. 'I haven't been back up. I've been doing this ever since he went.'

Prudence hoped the pattern was an easy one because Sally looked as though she hadn't stopped weeping for

hours. 'I've been thinking,' said Sally. 'Maybe he'll
come back.' She looked at the telephone, 'He might
ring.'

'He might,' said Prudence. 'But those who walk out
don't often walk back.'

'How would you know?' The tea was very hot.
When Prudence sipped it almost scalded her throat.
'Although I suppose you do,' Sally went on, 'you've
done it often enough.' She hiccupped, still on the edge
of tears, her lips trembling, 'I'm sorry, I didn't mean
to sound like that. I just wish I was more like you.
You never get hurt. Nobody will ever break your
heart.'

'I hope not,' said Prudence, and made herself smile.
She might have said that yesterday she met a man she
couldn't get out of her mind. And this morning she
had waited a little while, wondering if her phone
would ring.

Sally's heart would mend. It had done before, she
was in love with love. But sometimes, Prudence could
have told her, a woman loved and trusted a man so
much that most of her died if he went away. Nobody
would ever matter that much to Prudence. She would
never give any man the power to do to that to her.

'Come on,' she coaxed, 'drink up. Who knows what
the day will bring?'

The morning brought very little. Sally put on dark
glasses and went on knitting, and Prudence stayed in
the shop instead of going into her workroom because
Sally was in no state to deal with customers. The
phone rang several times and always Sally called from
the office, 'Please, would you——?' so that Prudence
always answered.

Sally waited, obviously holding her breath, until
Prudence indicated it was not Adrian. It was not Jason
Ballinger either. Prudence didn't expect Jake to ring.

He might phone her at home, she thought, but he wouldn't be chasing her at work during the day, he wouldn't be that eager. She didn't hold her breath at all.

Just before lunchtime a girl came in. She had bright eyes and a sharp face, and when she saw Prudence she asked, 'Is Sally around?' She had been one of the first to tell Sally that Adrian Foster was in a wine bar ten miles away with a blonde, when he was supposed to be working late. Her name was Lissa Harcourt, she worked in the same office block as Adrian, who thought he was God's gift to every woman he met, and she was sorry for Sally.

She had come to say that Adrian had gone up in the lift with two suitcases this morning and ask what was going on. 'Yes, she's in,' said Prudence. She was not over-fond of Lissa. She knew Lissa was Sally's friend, but she disliked Lissa's nose for gossip. 'She's in the office and she's feeling pretty low.'

'Oh!' Lissa's eagerness fell from her. 'Has he——? I mean——?'

'Left her?' said Prudence. 'Yes.'

'Poor Sal. Can I go in?' She sounded as though Sally was in intensive care, and Prudence smiled drily,

'So long as you're not going to say, I told you so.'

'Oh, I wouldn't!' Lissa was shocked at the thought, and indignant, 'As if I would! Can she come to lunch?'

'Good idea,' said Prudence. 'She might manage a little light nourishment.' Lissa gave her a reproachful look and went into the office, coming out with Sally a few minutes later. Sally was still wearing her dark glasses, but she was pleased to see Lissa who, Prudence was sure, had been very sympathetic.

'Prudence doesn't understand,' Sally had probably said. She paused at the door to say, 'If there's a call I'll be back in an hour.'

'There won't be,' said Prudence. It was no kindness, pretending Adrian might phone, but Lissa looked shocked again.

There was no phone call, but within five minutes there was Adrian himself. The shop was empty, and after a quick glance around he made for the stairs. 'Can I help you?' asked Prudence. This was Sally's usual lunch hour, one till two, the best time to come if you didn't want to see her, and Prudence didn't think Adrian was looking for Sally.

'Just fetching something.' His grin lacked his usual jauntiness, and she waited where she was while he ran upstairs. She was glad Lissa had collected Sally, otherwise there could have been another scene. Almost at once she heard him coming down again. 'Do you know what happened to my photograph?' he asked, and she gave a hoot of laughter.

'Now I've heard it all. It's in the bottom drawer of the small chest.'

She went across to a wall case containing one of her jewellery displays, and began to fiddle with it. Sally shouldn't be left with the photograph. She was sentimental enough to take it to bed with her, or sit staring at it when she was alone, and Adrian certainly admired his own face; but it was a bit thick coming back to collect his picture.

'It's a silver frame,' he said. He had the photograph now and the frame would be worth a few pounds.

'Good thinking,' said Prudence. 'I heard you were tight-fisted.'

He and Sally always went dutch, and it was Sally's flatlet and she did the shopping. 'Oh, get the heck out of my shop,' Prudence said wearily, and turned on her heel. The last thing she expected was that he would follow her, but he did, into the office.

'Nobody cares about my side of this, do they?' he said.

Prudence didn't. She was sure that Adrian was an expert in being misunderstood, but she felt she understood him. 'Sal's a grand girl,' he explained, 'but she stifles a man.'

Sally was a homemaker, loving and giving, and Prudence said, 'She loves you.'

'That's the trouble,' said Adrian. 'She wants to get married and spend the rest of her life hanging round my neck.'

'I shouldn't worry,' snapped Prudence. 'Married or not, I can't see you giving much support.'

She was sitting on the edge of the desk, in an attitude of natural grace because her body was lithe and slender, chin lifted, expression cool and contemptuous. As always there was that aloofness about Prudence Cormack, which had intrigued him from the first day Sally introduced them, here in the shop, just before he moved into the flat. She had beautiful skin, soft, and yet you felt there was steel in her, and he asked huskily, 'Has anyone ever told you how beautiful you are?'

'On your way, little man,' she said shortly. He was five foot ten, although he always described himself as six foot, and nobody had ever called him a little man before. She was a career girl, quick-witted, independent, and he thought, not for the first time, that she would be a damn sight more exciting than Sal.

'Sal's a drag,' he said. 'Not like you. You're my kind of woman.'

His sheer thick-skinned cheek should have been funny. She should have laughed at him, and told him what she thought of him, but she felt an appalling flash of rage that blotted out coherent thoughts. He had put down the photograph on the desk and her fingers closed on it, and she jumped to her feet and holding it in both hands hit him over the head with it.

She was as astonished as he was, and almost as scared. The glass shattered. She could have cut him to pieces. He whimpered, 'You bitch,' then screamed, 'What do you think you're doing? You're out of your bloody mind! You could have killed me. God, I'm bleeding—you've scarred me!'

He went to rush at her and she raised the frame again, with its jagged edges of glass. She wouldn't have used it again, but he wasn't to know this. It stopped him, a hand clapped to his cheek, and Jake Ballinger came through the open doorway from the shop. Ballinger must have heard the crash and the screaming, but probably not what preceded it. Prudence said, 'Out!' to Adrian, as if he was used to rough houses, and for all she knew he might be.

'Who the hell are you?' Adrian's voice was high and shrill, and Jake Ballinger seemed a head-and-shoulders taller, and a world tougher.

'The man from Rentokil,' said Jake, 'here to see to the rats.' Adrian edged through the door, watching both of them with wide scared eyes, and Prudence flung the photograph after him, not aiming it, just tossing it low with the caustic comment, 'You can still get your money on the frame. Don't go emptyhanded.' Adrian scooped it up and was out of the shop in a flash.

She was relieved to see nobody else in here. This kind of scene was hardly right for an up-market image, and she couldn't imagine how she could have explained it to her customers. Adrian Foster might need taking down a peg, but they wouldn't expect Prudence Cormack to be clouting him over the head.

She turned to Jason Ballinger, who hadn't turned a hair but was obviously waiting for her to say something, and when she gestured helplessly he suggested, 'A customer with a complaint?'

That made her smile faintly. 'You were right the first time,' she said. 'One of the rats. He's been living upstairs with a friend of mine who works here. This morning he moved out after a row and he's just called to collect his photograph—because of the silver frame and because he thinks he's beautiful—and he had the gall to tell me that Sal is a drag but that I'm his kind of woman.'

Jake laughed, 'Well, you've probably changed his mind on that!'

What have I done to your opinion of me? she thought. And to my opinion of myself. She hated the idea of losing control, hitting out instead of staying cool. She said, 'I didn't mean to smash the thing over his head.' There were shards of glass on the floor, looking razor-sharp, and she croaked, 'He said his face was bleeding. Did you see—any blood?'

'He'll live.' He sounded as though it was nothing much, and she asked wryly,

'Do you often hit people?'

'Not often. Do you?'

'Never. But he made me so angry. Sally's out to lunch now and as soon as she gets back she'll want to know if he's phoned, and if I tell her he's been to fetch his photograph she'll be in floods of tears all afternoon.'

'Not good for trade,' he said solemnly. 'Your friend sounds something of a liability.'

'She's very good for trade,' said Prudence. 'She's a lovely knitter. And she's a lovely girl, but unluckily for her she falls in love.'

It all sounded flippant, but Sally was suffering. 'I've got to take a suit out of the window,' Prudence said. This was a joke to Jason, Jake, whatever she should be calling him. He was cynical and worldly and he had walked into a ridiculous little pantomime and she would be able to smile about it herself in a little while. 'Be right back,' she said, and took a dress at random from the rail and carried it into the window.

Two women were looking in. As Prudence began to unpin the lilac suit they walked into the shop and one asked, 'Is it sold?'

'No, I was just changing the window.'

It took a little while, it was expensive, but after one of the women had tried on the suit, and walked around in it, and listened to her friend's opinion and asked Prudence what she thought, the sale was made. Prudence was on tenterhooks while they dithered. She was anxious to sell the suit, of course, but she was longing for them to go because Jake wasn't going to hang around for long, and he hadn't even told her why he was here yet.

Another girl was walking between the shelves holding a hank of pink wool, but Prudence slipped past her, into the office, where Jake was looking through the windows into the little yard where her car was parked. 'Sorry about that,' she said. 'Now what can I do for you? It isn't still the cottage, is it?'

'Certainly not.' She started to smile and when he went on, 'Will you have dinner with me tonight?' the smile widened, because she would have loved to.

'I'd have liked that very much,' she said, 'but it's Hallowe'en, and I'm going to a party and I promised to help. It's at Meon Farm, Jean's my oldest friend. Why don't you come? You'd be more than welcome.'

Jason Ballinger would be welcome anywhere, because he was very attractive and very rich. He'd have them flocking round, and Prudence would not be jealous because this was going to be a brief affair and because she was never jealous.

'No, thanks,' he said, and the customer with the hank of pinkish wool appeared in the open doorway and said, 'Excuse me, but I'm looking for this shade, but I'd like it with sparkle.'

Jake grinned at Prudence, 'Funny you should say that, that's what the man said.' He meant Adrian, who had decided that Sally was not exciting enough, Prudence realised, and she smiled back wryly. 'I'll be in touch,' said Jake, and the head of the girl with the wool swivelled to watch him go past her down the shop.

Prudence wanted to call him back and get their date fixed. But he was out into the high street before she could speak and she could hardly run after him.

'You want Glittersoft,' she told the customer, guiding her to a block of wools woven with bright metallic flecks, and opening the drawer beneath.

I want Jake Ballinger, she thought, and he wants me. She knew now that he must have felt the pull between them, just as she had, and that pleased her immensely. It gave her spirits such a lift that when Sally and Lissa came back from lunch she could hardly meet their eyes. She felt guilty about being happy, and it wouldn't have comforted Sally if she had said, This is quite different. I know the end of this already. It will only be skin deep and it will leave no scars, but for a little while it will be exciting and enjoyable.

'Did he——?' Sally ventured, and Prudence said, 'Sorry, nobody phoned.'

'I'd better tidy upstairs.' Sally climbed the stairs with dragging feet, but Lissa held back.

'She's coming home with me tonight,' she said when the door up there closed. Sally was supposed to be going to the Hallowe'en party, but she was hardly in a party mood, and Prudence said, 'That's nice of you. If she stays here she'll only be waiting for the phone to ring.'

'We all need friends,' Lissa announced, and Prudence nodded, remembering that when friends fell away the loss became almost unbearable. Sally's little tragedy had brought memories crowding back for Prudence, but she wouldn't dwell on them. They belonged to a life that was over and done with. 'Excuse me,' she said, and went into the office to dial the number of the wine merchants in the high street because she wasn't going to get out of here this afternoon by the looks of it, and she needed someone to bring round the rum for the punch and the two bottles of sparkling wine she was taking along to the party.

'Thank you,' she said, when the woman who answered the phone promised to see to that, and Lissa, who was still hovering said, 'There's a piece of glass on the floor.'

Most of it was in the wastepaper basket. Jake had picked it up while Prudence was selling the suit. She had thought it was all cleared away, she hadn't noticed the splinter that Lissa was gingerly fingering. 'Broken something?' Lissa enquired, and Prudence shrugged,

'He came back for his photograph, and I hit him over the head with it.'

'You *never*!' Lissa's eyes gleamed with admiration. She would never have believed that Prudence Cormack could get rattled enough to smash anything, much less over somebody's head. She giggled, 'I bet that gave him a nasty shock. Whatever did he do?'

It was dawning on Prudence that Adrian might well have tried to beat her up. Chivalry was not his strong point and she looked weaker than she was. 'Nothing,' she said. 'I was lucky. The Rentokil man called.'

Lissa giggled some more and asked, 'Have you got rats?'

'Not any longer,' said Prudence.

She wished Jake had agreed to come to the party. It would have created a stir if she had walked in with him, but that wasn't why she was sorry he wasn't coming. She would have liked to talk to him again, about anything, ask him all sorts of questions. She was consumed with curiosity about him as though it was important she should know even the unimportant things.

She didn't get into her studio that afternoon because Sally had developed a bad headache and Prudence gave her a couple of painkillers and made her lie down. She told anyone who asked for Sally that she had a migraine, and those who knew about Adrian weren't surprised.

Prudence helped knitters to wool and patterns, sold a jumper, and a bracelet and two pairs of earrings. She chatted and smiled with her customers, but she must have thought of Jake Ballinger at least fifty times. All the while there was this glow of excitement inside her. Life had been good to her in recent years. Nice things had happened, lots of nice things. But she couldn't ever remember feeling quite this way before.

She looked in on Sally, who slept for about an hour, and then lay with an eau-de-cologne soaked hanky across her brow. 'Thank you,' Sally said faintly as Prudence placed the hanky on her temples. 'You'd make a good nurse.'

'My mother had headaches,' said Prudence.

At five-thirty she turned the Closed sign on the door and went up to the flat again, made a cup of tea and took it into the little bedroom. 'Why don't you come to the party?' she asked.

'Oh no,' Sally whimpered. 'Suppose Adrian's there and he won't come home with me?'

He wouldn't come back, and it would be a nerve if

he showed up, because he had been invited as Sally's partner. 'I love him.' Sally had been lying here dry-eyed, but now the tears welled again and her voice took on a hopelessness that exasperated Prudence. 'I feel like nothing,' wailed Sally, 'as if everything's been taken away!'

'Stop that!' Prudence said sharply. 'That's a stupid way to carry on. You always give too much, but how can everything have been taken away when you're young and you've got your home and your job and your friends and your looks?' She glared at Sally, who began to blink and protest,

'You—don't understand.'

'And stop that too,' said Prudence. The cup was clattering in the saucer because her hand was shaking. She put it down and sat on the side of the bed with her arm around Sally's shoulders. 'I know I sound a hard-hearted-Hannah, but wailing and waiting's not going to help. Who *is* it?'

There was a tap on the door from the stairs to the living room, and Sally jerked forward craning to see as Prudence opened the door. 'Oh, Lissa!' moaned Sally.

'I think she should come to this party tonight,' said Prudence. 'Why don't you come too? The Howards wouldn't mind.'

'Fancy dress, isn't it?' said Lissa.

'Doesn't have to be,' said Prudence. 'The men are dressing in black, the girls are wearing what they like.'

'I can't go as a black kitten,' Sally sniffed. That was her costume, a cute kittenish little cat, and Prudence and Lissa exchanged glances.

'It would fit you,' said Prudence. 'Can she try it on?' Sally half nodded and Prudence reached down the box containing the velvet cat-suit from the top of the wardrobe. 'I'm a moon witch,' she told Lissa, and took out an Indian cotton dress in midnight blue, with a golden pattern, holding it up for Sally. 'You could deck yourself out in our jewellery and be another moon witch.'

'But—my face——' Sally muttered.

'You've got until eight o'clock.'

'I don't want——' Sally tried another appeal, but Prudence had Lissa on her side, because the party might take Sal's mind off things, and Lissa wouldn't mind going and the kitten costume would fit her. Lissa and Prudence both looked stern and Sally pushed her fingers through her hair and wailed, 'I'm a sight—look at my hair!'

'We'll put some heated rollers in,' said Lissa.

'Well, not that dress,' said Sally. 'It was his favourite—he chose it. I'll never wear it again.'

At last they found a dress that had no particular memories of Adrian, and Prudence brought up a pile of jewellery and left it with them. She had to go because she had to be early at the Howards'. 'Now you will see she comes, won't you?' she said to Lissa.

'We'll be there,' said Lissa.

'Suppose Adrian is?' muttered Sally.

'If he is I'll flatten him again,' Prudence promised, and she closed the door and hurried downstairs and out of the shop, leaving Sally bewildered and Lissa giggling.

Percy was waiting for her, as always padding around the house with her while she bathed and changed. Her dress was long-skirted in pearl grey chiffon, soft and floating, with full sleeves caught in at the wrists, round neck and narrow belt. It was quite plain but it showed the slender curves of her body and by the time she had added her jewellery the effect was exotic

Everything was silver, rings, bangles, chains, crescent moons dangled from her ears and stars shone in her dark hair. For everyday wear she would only

have worn a fraction of this, but she was satisfied
when she stood back from the mirror for a final
assessment. She was dressed for the party, and parties
at Meon Farm were always fun.

'I wish . . ' she sighed, talking to Percy as she always
did, 'I wish he was coming, don't I? If he doesn't
phone tomorrow, or I don't see him, I shall wander
over there when I get back from work.'

She had no more near misses while she was driving.
This morning had shaken her, she wouldn't let her
mind drift at the wheel again, but she still thought
about Jake. She would be going out to dinner with
him very soon, and she wondered where he would take
her. She probably knew the eating places around here
better than he did. If he asked her where she wasn't
sure whether she should go for the most opulent. He
was used to five-star treatment. Or somewhere small,
off the beaten track. She was looking forward to it and
she started planning what she would wear, the
questions she would ask him.

At the farm everything was almost ready for the
party. Lights were on, including floodlights that
bathed the ring of stones in an eerie glow. One of the
bigger barns was swept clean, with hay bales for seats
and pumpkin lanterns in alcoves and on cider barrels,
and the local group that would be providing the music
were plugging in and setting up their equipment. Jean
was in the kitchen and Prudence carried in her
baskets, with the three bottles and a tin of chocolate
bites.

Prudence was fond of all the Howards. This had
been one of the first houses to which she was invited
when she and her mother came to live here, and at one
time Jean had thought that Prudence and her brother
might make a match of it. Joe was keen, but Prudence
at twenty wasn't for settling down. She was opening

her shop and she didn't want to get serious with anybody. Now Joe was married, and Prudence was a friend whom Jean trusted completely. She was happily married herself and Prudence was down for one of the godmothers.

'Get you!' she shrieked as Prudence put down her basket and whirled about in all her silver finery. Jean's yellow smock billowed over her stomach and she grinned, 'I've just been asked if I'm supposed to be a pumpkin, but you look fantastic!'

'Everything but the kitchen sink,' Prudence joked. 'And Sally will be along festooned in another lot. Maybe we could flog some of it after they've all had a few drinks.' She laughed, then became serious. 'About Sally.'

Jean had heard about Adrian, mostly through Prudence, she didn't know Sally well, but she agreed that the break-up was sad and promised that Sally shouldn't be made to feel a wallflower.

What Jean *had* heard was that Jason Ballinger had taken Prudence round the conference centre yesterday. Before her baby was on the way she had been a member of the hang-gliding club herself, her brothers and husband still were. Joe had been one of those at the top of the hill yesterday when Bobby brought Prudence's glider back.

Now, while Prudence gave a trayful of tumblers a final polish with a soft cloth, Jean enquired, 'And how did you get on with Jason Ballinger?'

'Fine,' said Prudence, and held one tumbler up to the light, checking for smears although no one else was going to.

'What's it like now, the old hotel?'

'Very lush.'

'Did he ask you about the cottage?'

All the Howards thought Prudence should move

out. They were practical people, and it was a poky little house. 'Yes,' said Prudence, 'but I don't want to go.'

She really ought to tell Jean that Jake had arrived at the shop today and invited her to have dinner with him. They had always told each other about the men in their lives when they were girls, although Jean and the farmer's son from next door were obviously an ideal match. Prudence's confidences were more entertaining because Prudence never got too serious, Jean never had to worry about Prudence. Jean had thought it was a pity she hadn't married Joe, but Prudence wasn't a marrying girl, and Bobby Bygrave was a nice enough boy, but she couldn't see Prudence spending the rest of her life with him.

'Well, go on.' Jean urged. 'Tell me what he said.'

'He just showed me round,' said Prudence. She didn't want to talk about Jake and she didn't know why. 'Are you going to put all that into the punch?' she asked nodding towards the bottle in the basket. 'And where do you want these glasses?'

'In the barn,' said Jean. 'They're for the cider. Do you think there's enough food?' There were groaning trestle tables running the full length of the huge old farmhouse kitchen.

'Enough to feed an army,' said Prudence, beginning to add chocolate crisps to the dishes of cakes and candies.

The party was a success. It couldn't miss. Jean and her mother and her brothers' wives were all super cooks, so the buffet was superb. Everybody was here to have a good time and even Sally was smiling sometimes, and dancing.

Prudence danced. She was finding it a strain continually being questioned about Jason Ballinger. Nobody seemed to know he had been to her shop, but everybody had heard that he had shown her round his conference centre. His name came up constantly and there was nothing she had to tell. But when you danced you didn't have to talk.

The weather was kind, and the guests spilled between the house and the barn and around the circle of the stones. At midnight they would join hands and dance, snaking between the stones, singing old country songs, pretending this was some ancient ritual. It wasn't. The Howards had had Hallowe'en parties ever since Jean and her brothers were children, and the year before last Jean and Prudence had strung together the midnight chant which had been the hit of the evening. After all, it was Hallowe'en, and the site was ancient, and obviously a rite was called for.

Last year hadn't been so good because it had poured with rain, so that most of the girls broke ranks and scampered for shelter, leaving an almost entirely male crocodile, rushing round the stones, backed by a chorus from the barn. But tonight was fine and clear.

Prudence was dancing with Bobby as the witching hour neared. 'Do you want another drink?' he asked her.

'No, thanks, but you get one.'

She was under the stars, dancing, and when he came back he said without any preamble, 'I've just spoken to Sally. She says she never phoned you last night to say she was coming round.'

Prudence hadn't given that white lie another thought. She should have asked Sally to back her up. Now she could only say, 'No.'

'Why did you say she did?'

The music floating out from the barn was fainter than it had been, two of the group were taking a breather, and Bobby's voice was loud enough to make the dancers who were nearest turn to listen. They saw

a flushed-faced young man and Prudence looking
troubled.

'I'm not at all sure,' she said. Bobby was sure that
Prudence had told him that to get rid of him, to get
him out of her house, and he was indignant. 'You
could have asked me to go,' he told her. 'You could
have told me not to come. I don't hang around where
I'm not wanted.'

The cider was making him belligerent, he was on his
high horse, and there were grins around them. Bobby
was getting the brush-off—Prudence was at it again.
They were all in a mood when almost anything is
funny. 'I'm sorry,' said Prudence.

'The hell you are,' snapped Bobby, and marched
away to laughter.

Prudence danced on. She couldn't see what else she
could do. She *had* lied to get rid of him, although it
would have been just as easy to plead a headache. Only
she hadn't had a headache and she had been healthy
and hungry over the meal. It wasn't until he kissed her
and she kissed him back that she had known she could
not let the kissing go further. She had panicked and
babbled the first thing she could think of.

The music was a roll of drums and over the
loudspeakers they were exhorted to get into line.
Prudence caught hands with another couple and the
singing started, 'Here we go round the Standing
Stones, the Standing Stones, the Standing Stones,
here we go round the Standing Stones on a cold and
frosty evening. This is the way we greet the Stones,
greet the Stones, greet the Stones . . .' You bobbed
your head to each as you passed. It was all a laugh,
nothing like the old rituals with their dark and terrible
secrets. Floodlights spotlit the stones, throwing long
shadows and leaving the hill and the trees outside the
circle of light shrouded in blackness.

Of course you wished as you danced. Although nobody believed, ninety per cent of them were making a wish. Prudence was, and she had invented this. She wished for health and happiness, and she could guess what Jean was wishing as she bounced along, smiling at her husband. The wind seemed to be rising, lifting Prudence's hair; and she smiled—I wish for Jake Ballinger for a little while, just long enough to become good friends so that he never quite forgets me and so that I remember him.

The speed of music and dancing quickened, until most of them were falling about laughing, and only a final few were still hanging on, following the leader—at a fast gallop around the Stones. Jean had dropped out and so did Prudence, watching and laughing, hands on her hips, keeping well back from the circle.

She had wished to know Jake better so that she would remember him, but she thought she would remember him now, even if she never saw him again. He was as clear in her mind as though she had seen him daily for years. Seen him naked. Touched and tasted him.

A hand was on her shoulder and she turned her head. He stood in the shadows behind her, and she was surprised that her voice sounded so calm. 'You came to the party?'

'Only to fetch you away,' he said.

CHAPTER THREE

THE others at the party were still laughing and singing, but Prudence didn't look back and in the confusion nobody saw her go. Jake Ballinger drew her away, out of the lights into the shadows, through the trees and down the hill.

It looked weird from below. The lights on the stones up there, that could have been brightest moonlight, and the little dark moving figures, as though time had slipped back. But if the night had been that bright no one would have come out to dance for the old gods for fear of witch-hunters. Beside her Jake asked, 'What on earth is going on?' and she laughed, 'It's all right, it isn't a coven. We made it up a couple of years ago, and that's the nearest to an orgy there's going to be.'

She wondered how long he had stood there. Long enough to know this was just a party. 'Why are you all nodding at the stones?' he asked her, and she said,

'A little bow's a sign of respect. When they start nodding back we'll cut it out. How did you find me?'

She had told him where she was going, but there was quite a crowd. 'I followed your scent on the wind,' he said, and his hands slipped down to her waist, moulding her against him. A light touch, he was smiling, and Prudence looped her hands around his neck, head thrown back, smiling too, feeling a stirring of delight from his fingertips, as though wherever his hands moved her nerve ends would respond.

She could smell the cold air on his skin and she

thought, I could follow your scent. I could find you in a crowd. She said, 'My car's up there.'

'Mine's down here.'

They were nearer the bottom of the hill, and she had had several glasses of punch and she probably wouldn't have driven herself home tonight. 'Shall we take yours?' she said. 'Do you want to see my home?'

'I'd like that.'

Prudence usually got on well with people. She was kind and helpful so most people liked her; and she had style and sex appeal, so most men fancied her and some fell in love with her. That was nothing new. But now, with her hand in Jake Ballinger's, she ran down the rest of the hill, and the carefree feeling was new that she needed no defences because she was with someone she could trust completely. She had to remind herself that she had only known him for a day, not for years. But, as she waited for him to unlock the car, it seemed she couldn't recall a time without him.

Perhaps the punch had been stronger than she thought, although she had laced hers with lemonade. Or there might be a magic in the stones, perhaps she was under a spell. She got into the car, tucking her skirts around her ankles, turning to look as he climbed in and settled his long length behind the wheel. It was a strong profile, the big nose and the firm chin. His hair was ruffled, the dark tawniness looked almost black, like her hair, but his hands were darker than her skin. He reached to touch her cheek and leaned over to brush her lips, and his mouth was warm and familiar as though they had done this a hundred times before.

But there was nothing mundane about the caress. A little more pressure, a moment longer of contact, and the tingling would have run like sweet fire through all her nervous system. As it was it left her limp.

There was hardly a light burning down here. Jake

had parked in the road where the track led up to the farm. His was the last of a long line of cars and it would be hours yet before the others were driven away. They passed several that Prudence recognised, including Bobby's Capri, but it seemed right and proper that she should be leaving with Jake, that he should have come to fetch her away.

As they drove along he asked about the Howards—'Tell me about them,' and she said how nice they were. The men ran the family farm. Mr and Mrs Howard were second cousins, which was probably the reason that they all looked as if they had come out of the same mould. Jean, like her mother and father and brothers, was fair-haired and big-boned, with a fresh complexion and blue eyes.

Prudence always felt happy with them, but they were neither important nor rich and she couldn't understand why Jake Ballinger should find them fascinating. Jean's husband was wiry as a jockey and all their friends were wondering if the new baby would break the Howard tradition and be small and dark, but who cared except family and friends, and Prudence finished, 'Either way it will be a lucky child, they're a super family. But why are you interested in them? You're not after their land, are you?'

'You said they were your oldest friends.'

'Yes. Well?'

'So I'm interested in them,' he said.

That would just be flattery, but it was rather how she felt herself. She wanted to hear about the people he mixed with, especially those who mattered to him. 'And how did you leave your friend who's unlucky in love?' he asked.

Prudence didn't expect him to have any sympathy for Sally. Being jilted often seemed comic to outsiders, and Jake was tough all through, she was sure of that.

'She came to the party,' she said. 'Under protest, but she came, and thank goodness Adrian didn't turn up.'

'He could have a sore head.'

'He could. It's too much to hope he's left town.' This car purred like a great cat. She lay back in her seat and thought, I wouldn't mind where you were taking me.

'Where did you live before you came here?' he asked, and she watched the lane, edged with hedgerows, rushing at her. Nobody was taking her down that darker road of memory. 'Scotland,' she lied. 'Edinburgh. Where do you come from? Which was your home town?'

'Ever heard of Tremain in Cornwall?'

'I don't think so.'

'It's a pretty place, you'd like it.'

He didn't tell her any more, nor ask for further questions. Music she didn't recognise was playing softly, and she watched his hands on the wheel through slitted lids and the feel of him relaxed beside her, not touching her at all but knowing that if she moved she could brush against him, wrapped her in a lovely languor. I could fall asleep, she thought, feeling oh, so comfortable. Or if he stopped the car and really kissed me I could go up like tinder. She smiled and closed her eyes and listened to the music.

She opened her front door with the key she hid under a stone. She had left lights on, one in the kitchen, another on the landing so that it shone faintly through the curtains of a dormer window. The long-burning stove in the living room was closed, and she opened the doors and poked the slumbering log before she switched on a side lamp.

Jake had followed her into the room. He made it seem even smaller, his head almost brushed the ceiling, and she guessed he was wondering why she was determined to stay here. The tiny rose-patterned paper and the furniture made it attractive. Her chesterfield and two armchairs were cottage-chintzy, and she had a few antique pieces; a little walnut knee desk, a round rosewood table and three pretty rosewood chairs. But the room was small and the house was small, and he had already offered her more than it was worth.

Percy sat in his corner chair, and as Jake looked towards him Prudence warned, 'He doesn't like being touched. Usually he stalks out now. He doesn't like company either.'

She went across to the animal and stroked him very gently. 'He was wild. Still is, I suppose.' This time Percy was making no move to leave, although his green gaze was fixed unblinkingly on the man. Perhaps he felt that Jake should be watched, guarded against.

'How long have you had him?' Jake asked.

'Since he was a kitten.' Jake sat on the chesterfield and she joined him, and Percy went on staring at them. 'I used to put food and milk outside for him,' she went on. 'I did it for months, he was a scrawny little thing. I don't know what happened to the rest of the litter, and I could never get him to come into the house.'

That was strange. It explained some of her affection for the cat because it had made a bond between them. 'Until my mother died,' she said quietly. 'Just after that I was here alone one night, and I looked up and there he was.'

She had been lying right here on the sofa, so full of sadness and bitterness, and she had raised her head and the kitten had been there beside her. She said, 'It's been his home ever since.'

'Just you two?'

Her mother should have gone into hospital before. She had known about the lump, but she had told nobody until it was too late because she hadn't wanted to live. She could have been saved if she had thought her life worth saving.

'We lost my father before I came here,' said Prudence. 'I don't have any other family.' That was true. Everybody here had believed her mother was a widow, but when a man goes away and you never see him again or hear of him again, although you know he is probably still living the good life because he cheated so many friends, then so far as you are concerned he is surely lost.

'I'm sorry,' said Jake.

Prudence had never been tempted to tell anyone. It would have been like tearing open a healed wound, bringing back all the old pain, but he was looking at her with piercing eyes and she asked quickly, 'Do you have any family?'

'No.'

'Tell me . . .'

'No,' he said. 'Tell me how a girl as crazy as you can be called Prudence?'

That made her sit up and protest, 'I'm not crazy!'

'You bow to stones,' he said. 'You smash photographs. You drive like a maniac.'

Her licence was unblemished. She was a very safe driver. 'Who says . . .' she began, then remembered yesterday morning, and bit her lip. 'If you're talking about what I think you are, who told you?'

'Somebody coming to see me,' he said, 'said a white B.M.W. with more or less your number, driven by a girl with a pale face and dark hair, had come straight for him this morning on the main road just beyond Eyesford.'

She whistled soundlessly. 'Did he report me?'

'Not much point, he couldn't have proved anything, but you scared him witless. As he works for me I'd rather he kept his wits about him. Do you often drive like that?'

'Never,' she said.

'Like you never hit people? Yesterday was a day for firsts.'

'Yesterday,' she said, 'I was worried.' She couldn't tell him she had been thinking about him when she was driving to work, but he knew that she had troubles with her assistant. He would probably think that was why she had gone veering on to the wrong side of the road.

'Well, don't do it again,' he said, 'I don't want to lose you so soon.' She grimaced and he shook his head at her. 'Prudence! It doesn't suit you.' Nobody had any idea how well it suited her, how prudent she had been in the last eight years. 'Do you have another name?'

She should have said she hadn't, but she told him, 'Susanna, and I don't answer to it.' She had been christened Susanna Prudence and her father had called her Susie. Everybody had. She had been Susie Sinclair before the running started.

'Smile,' said Jake, and touched the sides of her lips with fingertips, lifting them a fraction in a mock smile that became real because she liked him touching her. He held her face cupped in his hands and asked her, 'Why can't I get you out of my mind?'

'Can't you?'

'Not for any length of time.' He was looking closely at her, studying her face. 'You know you're beautiful, of course. But the world's full of beautiful women, so what is it about you that bothers me?'

There had been a time when scrutiny like this

would have terrified her. She had been fifteen when she and her mother had returned from a holiday in the sun to the luxury home where Susie had lived all her life. They hadn't been met at the airport. They had come home by taxi, and the housekeeper couldn't say why Mr Sinclair hadn't met them. He hadn't been here since the day before yesterday, but his business took him around and he knew when their plane was arriving, and when he waved them goodbye he had kissed his wife and daughter and promised, 'Two weeks today, I'll be waiting.'

Her mother had laughed and said something must have held him up. He would be phoning the house any time now, in the meantime they would unpack and the cases were carried upstairs, and she took the mail with her that had arrived while they were away.

It was a beautiful bedroom. Everything was luxurious—they had always lived the good life. The furnishings were white and gold, and Priscilla Sinclair had sat down at a desk to glance through her letters. There was a photograph of her husband and daughter, taken a few years before, on the desk, and a bowl of creamy double freesias. Propped up against the bowl was a white envelope with her name in her husband's writing.

He often left notes. Priscilla was a gay and scatty woman and David Sinclair had been leaving notes for her all through their marriage. They were sometimes reminders about places she had to be, things she had to do. Sometimes just love notes. This one would be to say welcome home and how much he had missed her, and she laughed as she opened it.

Susie was sitting on the bed, reading a letter of her own from a school friend. She heard her mother laugh and she glanced up, and it seemed to her in after years that her mother never laughed again.

Susie saw her change and crumble as though she had received a death blow. And she had. The letter had said 'Forgive me and forget me.' That David Sinclair's finance firm was deep in the red. He was going away. Priscilla was still young and he was sure she would make a new life for herself, as he had to. Bless you both, the letter ended. That was his only mention of Susie, who picked up the note as her mother sat shivering, staring at it.

'He's dead,' her mother had sobbed, and it might have been easier if he had been, because very soon a heartless fraud was revealed. He had cheated almost everyone who trusted him—clients, friends; and he got away with it. He had obviously planned his move, covering his tracks, and the new life waiting for him would be cushy.

Priscilla Sinclair disintegrated. Her home, her car, everything had to be sold, her social circle had been her husband's business circle. Some of them blamed her for not knowing what was going on, some suspected she had known. She had lived through David and her lifeline went with him.

Susie had to leave her exclusive school, there was no question of private fees now, 'He won't come back,' Susie said. She had no friends in the new school, but they all knew who she was because, briefly, her father was notorious. From being one of the most popular girls she became a butt for bullying, her work suffered, all hopes of university or art college faded.

They moved several times in months, ending by renting a single room in a nearby town. Priscilla Sinclair was on tranquillisers and sleeping pills. She would sit for hours looking at her husband's photograph and asking Susie what she had done to deserve this. You loved him too much, Susie had thought. You should have loved yourself a little so that you could face life without him.

Nobody seemed to want them after David Sinclair's flight, and Priscilla Sinclair aged ten years in as many months. Then they had their first stroke of luck.

Priscilla's father had disapproved of her marriage. She had eloped, convinced that David would keep her safe and happy for ever, and her father had washed his hands of her. When the crash came he had not been charitable enough to offer them a house, although they were the only family he had, but dying he had willed most of his money to various charities. And some to Susie.

It was far from a fortune, but it seemed a lot to the girl. She had just left school and she told her mother, 'We're leaving here. We're going to start a fresh life where nobody knows us and nobody blames us.' They *were* blamed. Their carefree past was held against them, and Susie too had aged and changed. She changed their name, to her mother's maiden name, and she never wanted to hear anyone call her Susie again.

She took her mother on holiday to a quiet hotel in a quiet seaside resort, and tried to nurse her back to health. But the heart had gone out of Priscilla. She was bereaved and she mourned her dead, although she loved the girl who was now called Prudence, and when Prudence found the house she wanted Priscilla came to the village and could have made friends. She was well liked. She was a sweet sad lady. None of them would have believed that a few years before she had laughed so much, and wanted to live for ever.

In the early days Prudence was afraid of being recognised. If she caught anyone staring at her she had tensed and turned away, but that was a long time ago. Before she was out of her teens she had shed all resemblance to the girl who had been Susie Sinclair. Susie had been plump with a mop of short dark curls

and a round smiling face. If the old life had continued
she would obviously still have changed, grown tall and
slender as she shed the puppy fat, her face would have
matured from a pretty youngster to a fascinating
woman. But the new life changed the woman inside.
No one would ever see Prudence Cormack now and be
reminded of Susie Sinclair, and now she could look
into Jake's eyes and say gaily, 'I'm sorry I bother you.'

'Don't apologise. I enjoy a conundrum.' He leaned
back, smiling at her. 'I'd like to know you better—
much better. For instance, do you often wear your
entire stock?'

She was really done up like a Christmas tree. 'Only
when I'm a moon witch,' she said.

'Of course. Would you consider dispensing with
some of it?' Bangles snaked up her arms, and chains
galore hung round her neck. 'Only it makes it a little
difficult to know where to put the hands.'

She wasn't exactly encased, but anyone holding her
without due care might get scratched. 'Where were
you considering putting them?' she enquired, eyebrows
raised in an expression of mild interest.

'We could start with the rings,' said Jake. She had
them on every finger, and she took them off, slowly,
one by one, dropping them on the carpet by the sofa.
Then he reached and held a hand, and unclasped a
bracelet, eased off another, and lifted the star clips out
of her silvered hair. Prudence took the chains from
around her neck, except for the little moon that she
always wore. The crescent moon earrings still swung
and he said, 'Moon witch—that suits you.'

'But not a name for everyday wear.' She smiled.
'Prudence suits me. If you get to know me better
you'll believe me.'

Stripping off the jewellery had been like being
disrobed, undressed, and now it would have been easy

to slip out of her dress, but it would have been too soon. Maybe they would make love before Jake went away, she didn't know yet, but she thought she knew herself. 'Another thing I told you,' she said. 'I'm not a melting lady.'

But when he kissed her she felt the intensity of it like an electrical charge that jerked her head back. He could melt her. There could be a fusion here that would be white-hot, and she was not risking that.

She forced a laugh. 'I don't think my cat trusts you!' The cat had been watching the glitter of silverware, falling on to the carpet. Its eyes glittered and Jake said, 'I bet he's good with the rats.'

'Are you a rat?'

'Not me. I'm the good guy, remember?'

Prudence smiled for real then and thought, we could have fun, laugh together. Her hand was trailing over the edge of the sofa and she scooped up some chains lifting them. 'Samples,' she said. 'They'd go well in the boutique in the Conference Centre. Cheap and cheerful or exclusives.'

'You do have a cash-register mind,' he smiled with her, but that wasn't true. She was bright in business, but she was no grabber. He knew that she was joking her way out of a situation that was rapidly reaching the point of no return. Not tonight, she was saying, but thank you all the same.

They looked at the jewellery. Still joking at first. Prudence picked up a bracelet with star signs in small white glittering stones as they would appear in a clear night sky, and said, 'These go well. Zodiac, you know. You could take some of these, couldn't you?'

'Depends on the price.'

'Well, it would, and you'd drive a mean bargain.' But in the end she was showing him her work because he thought it was beautiful. Soon she was telling him where her ideas had come from, piece after piece, as he held them in his hand, looking at them, listening to her. Whether local crafts would eventually be on sale in the Conference Centre was immaterial. What mattered was that Jake said they were beautiful and that she was talented, and he wasn't flattering her. They sat quietly together talking until a clock struck one and she asked, 'Do you want some coffee?'

'I think I'd better go.'

'Yes,' she said, and then they were smiling again.

'You're not going to show me round.' No question, a statement. Down here he could see at a glance that there was only kitchen, bathroom and living room. Upstairs two bedrooms led from the top of the narrow stairs, and she was not taking him upstairs.

She went out to his car with him and he said, 'I'll be back tomorrow night. Can you break any date you have?'

She had none, but if she had she would still have said yes. 'What time?' she asked.

'Eight?'

'I'll be here.'

He didn't kiss her again. He got into the car and sat for a moment at the wheel, his face as impassive as a Red Indian chief's. Then he grinned, raised a hand in farewell, and backed out of her small drive, to go along the road and up the much grander drive to the Conference Centre.

Prudence watched the lights of his car take the bend and sweep up and round the back of the house. If she stayed out here longer she would see windows illuminated, and she could follow his progress in her mind's eye through the great echoing building. He didn't mind being alone. It would give her the shivers, all by herself in there, and it was crazy feeling she knew him so well when really she hardly knew him at all.

Percy vanished into the night and she went back into Stable Cottage. The name was apt, because it had once been part of the stables, but it summed up all the house meant to Prudence. It was her sanctuary, sound and solid. When she had come to it, opening the door with her own key, shutting it behind her, she had promised herself that she and her mother had done with running. Here they were safe. And they had been, although her mother had been dying ever since she read that note.

That had been terrible, but life here had been good for Prudence. The little house was more than bricks and mortar to her, and although she might leave it some day she would be apprehensive when she did. She couldn't tell them that, not even Jean, because it sounded silly and it would have meant talking about her father.

She gathered up the jewellery and packed it for taking back to the shop tomorrow, and wondered how the party at Meon Farm was progressing. Parties there usually ended with a cooked breakfast for the hardier guests, and someone would probably have started looking for Prudence by now. Her car was still parked in front of the farm, she would have to cycle up to get it in the morning. But eventually it would be obvious that Prudence had skipped, and later she would have to explain. 'Jake Ballinger came to get me.'

That would cause talk. That would give them something to think about. It was giving her something to think about herself, as she got out of the grey chiffon dress to get ready for bed. She had met a man who was dynamite, mentally and sensually. Who couldn't get her out of his mind, he said, which could make the next month or so quite eventful.

She was vigorously brushing the silver glints out of her hair when the phone rang, and she hesitated, because this could be Bobby. Even if it was somebody who wouldn't be angry; who just wanted to know how she had left the party, she didn't want to start telling them this late.

'Hello,' she said at last.

'Goodnight,' said Jake. She knew his voice at once and again he was vividly with her. 'Goodnight,' she said, and she thought he put the phone down when she did. She stood, with her hand still on the receiver, tracing the spine of it with a fingertip as though she stroked a man's hand, and thought, when the final goodbye comes I must be the one to say it.

At least it wasn't raining next morning when she got the old bike out of the garage. She had bought that the first year she came here for cycling to the Poly. She still used it sometimes for getting around the lane's but she rarely took it into town, and by the time she had climbed the hill to the farm she was going to be out of breath and windblown.

Percy saw her off, as usual, as she left home half an hour early, and just before Eyesford she heard the drone of a helicopter overhead. That had to be Jake, and here was a situation that summed it all up: him helicoptering off and her peddling away. She could imagine him looking down and smiling. She was on a clear straight downhill road, and for a few seconds she took her feet off the pedals, swooshing down, freewheeling like a small boy playing the fool. Then she started back-pedalling and waved.

That meant, I see you, and I'll see you tonight, and enjoy your day; and the helicopter turned and she knew that he had followed, looking for her, and that if she had waited a little longer he would have driven her to the farm to collect her car. She would have arrived there with Jake Ballinger and then nobody would believe they hadn't spent the night together. Whatever he had in mind was not a hole-and-corner affair. It would be temporary all right, but he didn't care who knew about it.

There were no cars parked in the road by the track to Meon Farm now, and Prudence's was the only vehicle in front of the farm except for the family Range Rover. The house was a sprawling old building. Jean's husband helped to farm the adjoining land that he would inherit one day, but he and Jean and their children would probably go on living here until that day came. They had their own rooms and Jean cooked in the family kitchen with her mother.

They were in the kitchen now and when Prudence knocked on the back door Jean opened it. She looked brighter-eyed than most of the party guests would be, because she had watched her drink and diet carefully, but she was yawning. 'The last of 'em have just gone,' she informed Prudence. 'It was a good do, wasn't it?'

'Terrific,' said Prudence. 'I've got to get to work now, I've just come for the car.'

'Cup of tea? We're just sitting down to one.'

'Why not?' Work was waiting, and maybe the shop wouldn't open at nine if Sally had gone home with Lissa. But whenever she turned up Sally would still be fretting about Adrian, and I could do with a strong cup of tea before I face that, thought Prudence, following Jean into the kitchen.

The dishwasher was on, but there were still piles of plates and stacks of glasses waiting. Mrs Howard was putting a patchwork tea-cosy on top of the tea-pot and she beamed broadly when she saw Prudence. Mrs Howard never seemed to change. She was a big happy motherly woman, a farmer's daughter, a farmer's wife, like Jean. One day Jean would look like her.

Mrs Howard had always been fond of Prudence, from the first day Jean brought her home from college. She had thought the girl's eyes were too big for her face, and that she needed feeding up and she had set about feeding her, although Prudence put on no weight. She still urged extra helpings of pudding whenever Prudence came to dinner.

Jean sat down now, adjusting her bulk to the chair, and enquired, 'And where did you vanish to last night?'

'Home,' said Prudence, maddeningly, because that wasn't the answer Jean was after and she wasn't getting away with that. Mrs Howard put out another cup and saucer and Jean began to pour the milk, demanding, 'Who took you? It wasn't Bobby—I heard about that spat with Bobby, and he was still here looking down in the mouth a long time after you'd gone.'

Prudence pulled a wry face, and Jean had been half expecting this because Bobby Bygrave was very keen on Prudence, and Prudence always got restless when there were signs of a friendship becoming a commitment. Some girls, like some men, just weren't the marrying kind.

'It was Jake Ballinger,' said Prudence, and Jean nearly spilt the milk. She gasped, 'You mean Jason Ballinger? *The* Jason Ballinger?'

'I don't think there are two of them,' said Prudence.

'I'm pretty sure there aren't two,' croaked Jean. 'I didn't see him around.'

'Well, he just sort of popped up from behind a tree.'

'Come for you?'

'So he said.'

'And you just sort of went off with him?'

'Sort of, yes.' Mrs Howard was pouring the tea into the milk, watching Prudence with a worried look, but Jean and Prudence were sharing this joke between them. 'Well,' Prudence went on, 'when he was showing me around his place yesterday I suggested a small boutique with local crafts that the folk who came for the conferences might buy, and he was interested in my jewellery.'

Jean pealed with laughter, 'And you were wearing most of it!'

'By a lucky fluke I was,' said Prudence with mock solemnity, and it was no good saying, 'He just looked at the jewellery and then he went'; because Jean wouldn't believe her. 'When did Sally go?' she asked.

'I don't know.' Jean turned to her mother, who shook her head, and Prudence felt that was disapproval for her as well as disclaiming any knowledge of Sally's departure. 'Not too late,' Jean added. 'They weren't here for breakfast.'

'I'd better be off. I've probably got to open up,' and Prudence gulped down her tea. There would be more questions from Jean, out of her mother's hearing, and when Prudence put down her cup she said to Mrs Howard, 'It was a lovely party—but then they always are.'

For Christmases, birthdays, celebrations, the Howards had friends whose families had known their family for generations, and Prudence was grateful at being included. When Jean had her baby and Prudence was a godmother then she really would be part of the family.

'And you know you're always welcome here,' said Mrs Howard. She wasn't smiling and she sounded serious, and Prudence said, 'Thank you,' as Jean said, 'I'll see you to the car. Don't forget the keys.' They hung on a hook on the dresser.

As soon as the kitchen door closed Jean said excitedly, 'He must have been mighty struck with you. You didn't say anything about him coming.'

'I honestly didn't know. I did ask him and he said no.'

'Then he changed his mind.' Jean rolled her eyes. 'He must have been thinking about you.'

'I suppose he must.' He had said he couldn't keep her out of his mind for any length of time. Prudence had left her bike propped up against the wall by the back door and they walked across to where her car stood.

'Hey,' said Jean, 'keep me posted. I need a bit of excitement—I'm not getting much these days.' Her smile was contented, but she enjoyed hearing about Prudence's lively life.

'It won't be for long.' Prudence got into the car. 'The place opens for business in the new year and he'll be away to fresh woods.'

'So make the best of the next——' Jean ticked the months on her fingers, 'November, December, maybe January. Nearly three months.'

'Maybe I will,' laughed Prudence, and Jean went smiling into the kitchen where her mother drained a cup of tea, sighed and shook her head again. 'He isn't married or anything,' Jean said defensively. 'And Prudence isn't going to lose her heart to him because he's only here for a few weeks. Jason Ballinger's a tycoon, a high flyer.'

'Is he?' Mrs Howard went to the sink. She still didn't entirely trust dishwashers, although this one had been in her kitchen for over a year. She found a smear of fried egg adhering to one plate now and turned on the tap and started whisking up a bowl of soapy water. 'So Mr Ballinger's a high flyer? Well, I only hope that Prudence isn't trying to fly too high herself!'

There was no Sally in the shop when Prudence opened up and she ran upstairs to tap on the flatlet door. When she got no answer she looked in and Sally obviously had not returned here last night. Prudence expected that, Lissa had said Sally would be going home with her.

There were a few letters, all business, personal mail rarely came here, and Prudence opened them and made notes. She brushed her hair into its usual deep waves, and she looked neat and bright and ready for business. Ready for anything. Preferably customers, of course, but if Adrian had swaggered in or the Vatman had called she felt more than capable of dealing with either. She was filled with gaiety this morning, and her first customer, a middle-aged woman who came to buy some wool to make a cardigan took Prudence's advice and went out with a pretty harebell blue, the colour of her eyes, that was going to turn into the most successful garment she had ever made.

Prudence picked out a sweater for herself. It was some time since she had treated herself to any clothes, and the nip in the air meant that colder weather was coming. This was in soft mohair, with a pattern of white clouds and birds on a blue sky. She set the sweater aside and made two business phone calls, and one to the timber mill to arrange for a load of logs to be delivered to Stable Cottage, and the next time the bell rang over the shop door Sally walked in.

She was carrying an overnight bag and wearing a mac over the dress she had worn last night. She still looked washed out, but she did try to smile as Prudence came out of the office. 'I suppose there've been no calls for me,' she said.

'Not since I got here.'

'Sorry I'm late.'

'That's all right. We've only had one customer in.'

'I stayed with Lissa's people.' Sally hesitated at the bottom of the little staircase. 'I'd better get changed, but——' her voice was unsteady, 'I'm dreading going up there. I mean, everything's going to remind me.'

It reminded Prudence of her mother, but Sally was young, she didn't have her whole life invested in Adrian, although she was going to need help getting over him.

'How about us changing the flat around?' Prudence suggested. 'We could redecorate for a start. There are such pretty papers, and you could get some curtains to match.' Prudence had learned interior decorating by trial and error in her own home. She had helped Jean prepare her rooms in Meon Farm when she married. She did most of the decorating here and she could have Sally's flatlet transformed in a few hours. 'I'll help you,' she offered. 'We could do it tomorrow afternoon.'

They closed half-day on Wednesday, so after a token protest Sally went up to change her dress for a jumper and skirt and then went into the shop next door to look at wallpaper patterns. When she came back from the shop carrying two huge pattern books she said, 'You didn't tell me you were nearly in an accident yesterday.'

Sally had just heard that Prudence had been white as a sheet when she'd arrived for work and she had told Sarah Dandy that she had just missed a crash. That was a slight exaggeration, although she had been shaking. 'It was only a skid,' she said.

'I was so upset myself,' said Sally, 'I hardly saw you. Gosh, if anything had happened to you yesterday, it would have done for me!'

'It happens all the time,' said Prudence. 'Near misses in cars.' It was the first time she had found herself on the wrong side of the track heading for another motorist, but she had met many a one hogging her road space. Yesterday she had been driving like an

idiot, and she started to say, 'It was my——' but Sally
was saying earnestly, 'I don't know what I'd do
without you. You're such a good friend, and as long as
I've got friends things could be worse, couldn't they?'

'They could,' agreed Prudence.

'Lissa told me you hit him—Adrian.'

'Yesterday,' Prudence murmured, 'was a day for
firsts.' Remembering Jake's words made her smile.
'Let's have a look at these patterns.'

Sally made her selection sadly, but it was giving her
something else to think about, and when anyone came
into the shop who knew the girls personally Prudence
showed them the books so that Sally received plenty of
advice. It was better than too much sympathy and just
as supportive. Lissa arrived at lunchtime and by then
the choice had been narrowed to two, and she went up
to the flatlet with Sally to hold the books up and get
an idea of the designs in situ.

The phone rang while they were up there and when
Prudence answered Jake said, 'Hello.' She knew his
voice from the one word. Like last night's goodnight.

'So what's this about?' she asked.

'Just making sure you don't forget me.'

'That's not too likely.'

'What are you doing?'

'Answering the phone. Waiting for someone to
come in and buy.'

'Not designing your jewellery?'

'Not today. Sally's still convalescent. What are you
doing?' It was crazy, this sort of small-talk with a man
who was worth millions, chatting as though he had a
little shop like hers.

'I've just come from a meeting,' he said.

'Did it go well?'

'Oh yes.' There was a touch of grimness in his voice
now, but satisfaction too, and Prudence could imagine

a panelled room, a long polished table with him sitting at the head. 'What are you doing this evening? Do you want to eat out?'

She was sure he had been giving his opinions at that meeting and not taking much notice of anybody else's, but now he was asking for hers. What did she want to do? If they didn't go out there was her cottage and the empty Conference Centre, with beds in both and long settees, and the almost certain prospect of lovemaking. She was not sure about that, so soon. She felt that it would be dangerous, and that afterwards she could regret it bitterly.

She needed time to think and she intended taking her time. 'Let's eat out,' she said. 'On a Tuesday night and off-season we can get in anywhere. How about the Fourways?'

That was a small hotel, on a crossroads at the end of the village, that had a good carvery, and she suggested it because it was near, you could walk to it. It wasn't going to impress Jason Ballinger, but there was nothing wrong with the Fourways.

'Whatever you want,' he said. 'I'll see you at eight.'

It wasn't generally known yet that she was dating him. Jean might have mentioned it, but she was a girl who never had gone in for gossip. Prudence almost told Sally. Then she thought, I will tomorrow, after this evening. I'll tell her then, but I mustn't sound too happy and I must stress that it's very a casual affair. The best that can come out of it is friendship. Even when he went away she thought they that might still be friends, and the idea pleased her.

The firm that was handling the decor in the Conference Centre was still at work when she got home. She could see their vans and she almost strolled over to see what progress had been made since Sunday. Everything was on schedule she knew. The staff that had been recruited locally were starting work on New Year's Day and would be going in towards the end of next month to get the feel of the place and learn the scope of their duties.

That wasn't so long away, when you thought about it. Jean had joked that Prudence had the best part of three months before Jake left here, but really it was only weeks before she would have to settle for maybe a letter sometimes or a phone call. She would have to be very careful indeed that she wasn't left needing a great deal more than that.

She went into the house and changed and waited. It was dark when she heard the helicopter, and she thought, I hope he knows how to get that thing down in the dark, then she said to Percy, 'I'm going bonkers. Of course he does. I reckon he's pretty nearly indestructible.' The cat looked steadily at her and she thought she wasn't really talking nonsense because she did feel that Jason Ballinger was the strongest man she had ever met. Before she had met him she had been prejudiced, because once her father had been in big business. Not to the same extent as Ballinger and Merrick Enterprises, but biggish, and beneath the pretence of caring he had been heartless. But Jake was nothing like her father. He was like nobody but himself, and she looked at the clock that said a quarter to eight, and knew that he would be here at the time he had told her. If he ever pronounced, 'Two weeks' time, I'll be waiting for you,' he would be waiting.

He knocked on the door a couple of minutes to eight and she called, 'Come in.'

Percy got off the chair and was stiff-legged and claws at the ready when Jake came into the living room. 'Are you sure he's under control?' Jake queried, as Percy began to skirt the skirting board to get out.

Predence laughed, 'Just—don't touch.'

'I've no intention of touching,' he assured her, and Percy shot through the kitchen and the cat flap in the door. She went on laughing.

'Don't take it personally. Don't let it put you off all four-footed things.' She picked up her purse and she was ready to go.

'Are you for touching?' he asked, and she stopped laughing but went on smiling.

'A little.'

He kissed her very gently, his lips brushing her cheek and her mouth, as she stood holding her purse behind her. She had to grip the purse to stop herself pulling him close, and when that was all he did, bending a head to kiss her, she was left feeling hollow with longing.

'I don't know if you know the Fourways,' she began to chatter as they walked together out of the cottage. It wasn't the village pub, it was a small hotel with a public bar, but even if he had never been inside he must know of it.

'I haven't eaten there,' he said. 'Do we walk?'

'It's a nice night.'

'It is.' He slipped her hand through his arm. He was wearing a tan leather jacket, soft and supple. She could feel the muscles beneath it and even in the pale light of the few street lamps he looked tanned and virile. I'll bet this is draining all the colour out of me, she thought, but as long as I hang on to you I'm in the glow of some of your energy and vitality.

She grinned, and he asked, 'What's the joke?'

'You look so healthy you make me feel anaemic!'

'Don't worry,' he said, 'I'll keep you warm.'

You do, she could have said. Walking with him quickened her heartbeats and made her skin tingle, and it was amusing to be recognised by the people she met. They didn't meet many—a few dog-walkers, a few heading for the pub. Prudence was a familiar face, but they most of them seemed to recognise Jason Ballinger too, and they were all surprised to see Prudence's hand through his arm.

She joked, 'There's going to be gossip about this,' after they left a couple of ladies goggling, and he asked, 'Do you mind?'

'I'm used to it. It's a village, and people talk because everybody knows everybody. They're talking about you anyway, because you've stirred things up.' She smiled. 'And they can talk all they like about me. I've never had much to hide.' She was speaking as Prudence Cormack whose life was an open book, although there were those who wondered why she couldn't keep a man. In fact she had never lost one. It had always been Prudence who walked away.

Jake asked about her day, and she told him they were giving the flatlet where Sally had lived with Adrian a face-lift. Tonight Sally and Lissa were doing the preparing and tomorrow afternoon when the shop was shut Prudence and Sally were putting on paint and paper.

'You must consult our designer,' he said, and she laughed.

'You've got to be joking. It isn't the place for gold leaf. You could put the whole flat into the shallow end of your swimming pool.'

There was a hush when they walked into the foyer, which connected with the bar by an archway. Everyone turned to look at them, and Prudence waved and called hellos, then they followed the manager into the dining room.

Only two other tables were occupied, but the carvery board was packed with joints of beef and pork, poultry and vegetables. They helped themselves and sat down. Jake ordered wine and Prudence saw the

diners watching them. She knew the four farthest
away, but the man and woman at the nearer table were
strangers to her. She often got admiring glances
herself, and with Jake Ballinger she realised that she
was half of a very eye-catching couple. She was a
pretty girl, but he was a man who would turn heads
anywhere. The pair over there might not know who he
was, but they knew he counted, and the woman
thought he was sexy. Prudence felt quite sorry for her
escort, because every time she glanced towards that
table the woman was looking wistfully towards Jake.

He never looked at anyone but Prudence. His
attention that night was entirely fixed on her, which
was flattering and fun. He asked her about her life and
her friends and she answered what she could, making
it up further back, skirting that. She had told him she
came from Edinburgh, which wasn't true, although
that was where her mother's father had lived, and
when he enquired where the house was she pulled a
face, protesting, 'What are you doing? Compiling a
dossier on me?'

'Getting to know you.'

'So tell me about you,' she said, and she thought the
keen taut face didn't tell much, even when he was
smiling. He did talk about himself, after a fashion. He
told her how he started with an old school in Tremain
which he converted into apartments. Other properties
followed and bigger projects. Some were sold outright,
others leased, until now, Ballinger and Merrick,
growing and spreading on an international scale, was
an empire, and the man who headed it was a powerful
figure.

But he talked about his achievements in a self-
mocking way, making Prudence smile, and occasionally
pealing with laughter. He was a stimulating conversa-
tionalist, he kept her talking too, trotting out her

opinions, discussing her likes and dislikes in everything from politics to pop. She couldn't remember a more enjoyable meal, although it wasn't the food, it was the company. She could hardly believe how fast the time had passed. She realised that the room was empty, except for the manager, and that the dregs of her third coffee were cold in her cup.

Jake signalled and the bill came on a salver, and the manager smilingly presented Prudence with a single carnation. That was the gimmick of the house, every lady eating here got a flower. Prudence had been here a number of times before and gone away with her bloom, and she thanked him, breathing in the perfume, hoping the flower would last when she got it home because it was a souvenir of a lovely evening.

The night struck surprisingly chill outside after the heat of the dining room and they walked quickly, Jake's arm around her. This was a real drop in temperature from last night, and they strode out down the empty street, not saying much after Prudence's gasp of, 'It's cold enough for snow!'

It would be warm in the cottage. She would stir up the fire and she hoped that Percy would restrain his anti-social instincts because she would be taking Jake in tonight. They could talk some more at least and see how the talking developed.

She opened the front door with her key and frowned. She thought she had left the usual lights on, in the kitchen and one upstairs, but the kitchen door was shut and there was a glow from the living room. Maybe she had overlooked that. She took the few steps down the little hall and drew in her breath sharply as Bobby got up from the chair by the fire.

He knew where she kept her spare key, but he had no right to let himself into her home, and she demanded furiously, 'What's all this about? What do you imagine you're doing here?'

She knew as she asked that someone had told him who she was with tonight, but when he sneered, 'It doesn't take much imagination to guess what you and your friend propose doing!' her face flamed. She was speechless for the moment as embarrassment choked her, then Jake stepped into the room and Bobby said,

'I don't believe I know you.'

Of course he knew. He had said hello to Jake on Sunday. He had been told who Prudence was with tonight. He had been sitting here waiting to tell her to get lost and wish Jason Ballinger the best of a bad bargain. 'But——' he began, and Jake said quietly,

'No reason why you should, but you will from now on, won't you?'

It wasn't just height. Jake was taller, his shoulders were broader, but Bobby was quite an athlete himself; and yet when Jake spoke a muscle twitched in Bobby's cheek and he swayed back a little as though he was expecting a blow. Prudence couldn't get out a word. Without moving or speaking, just by standing there, hands in his pockets, face expressionless, Jason Ballinger cut Bobby down, and Prudence thought, I was right, he could be a killer.

She managed to say, 'Please go,' and Bobby snarled, 'You're talking to me, of course!' and marched out.

She was sorry for Bobby, she blamed herself, and she had just glimpsed the ruthless side of Jason Ballinger when he had looked at Bobby with eyes as cold as ice. He looked at her now and said, 'If he has a key I should ask him for it.'

'He doesn't. He must have let himself in with the one I hide under a stone.'

She went to open the kitchen door to see if Percy was home and the cat came to meet her across the flagstones, letting her pick him up and carry him into the living room, and she resisted an impulse to hold him very tight.

Jake was still in the living room, he hadn't sat down, and he smiled at her with her cat in her arms, and he looked a different man. 'Are you trying to tell me something?' he asked.

Percy welcomed nobody, although Prudence hadn't carted the cat in as protection. She had just wanted her pet, and a few moments to compose herself. She was steadier now, and the idea of her fetching Percy to see Jake off made her smile. 'Well,' she said, 'maybe there is something I should say.'

If Bobby had not been waiting, changing the mood of the evening, it would have ended differently, but now her mind was cool. 'Bobby seems to have definite ideas on what's happening between us,' she told him, 'but I hope you haven't, because I've had a pleasant evening and you're an attractive man, but I don't like being hurried or hassled.'

'Who's hassling you?' he said. Although she was still nursing the cat he kissed her lips, as gently as the last time. 'I'll see you tomorrow.'

Prudence let him leave, and she was grateful to Bobby because she did need a little more breathing space and Jake hadn't taken umbrage. She let Percy jump down then, and the cat patted something lying on the floor and began playing with it, and Prudence realised that she had dropped her flower earlier. She rescued it from the cat's claws. It was crushed and the petals were falling—so much for my souvenir, she thought, but she couldn't throw it away. She carried it into the kitchen and floated it in a little bowl of water, smiling wryly at herself, because that was one of the most sentimental things she could ever remember doing.

CHAPTER FOUR

'I HAD dinner with Jason Ballinger last night,' Prudence said casually and Sally said, 'Who?'

Sally was still depressed. If Prudence had said 'Paul Newman' it would probably have got the same blank reaction. And Sally lived in the town. She wasn't much concerned with the conversion of an old house in a village eight miles away, although she did think that Prudence could be making a mistake, refusing the offer for her cottage.

'Ballinger and Merrick and they're building the Conference Centre just behind me,' Prudence explained, and then Sally showed a little interest.

'Did he want to talk about your house?'

'Never mentioned it,' said Prudence. 'No, he showed me round the place on Sunday and last night he took me out to dinner.'

'What's he like?'

'Pretty exceptional,' and Sally giggled and asked,

'Which?' It was the first glimmer of humour she had shown since Adrian left her, and Prudence laughed as though it was very witty.

'Not pretty, no. More hatchet-faced. But he's exceptional all right.'

'You are lucky,' said Sally wistfully, and then Prudence had to stress that nothing much could come of this because Jason Ballinger would be leaving soon.

This morning Sally was facing the customers on her own again and carrying on with her knitting in the intervals between. Incredibly she hadn't done a stitch wrong while she was knitting through the tears, and that sweater was almost finished. She sat on her usual chair by the window and started her needles clicking, while Prudence went into her studio workroom and spent most of the morning on her glitter zodiac jewellery. It was a good gift line and Christmas was coming.

She wondered what Jake's star sign was, and decided Taurus or Leo. She wondered if he would wear a medallion if she gave him one, and thought he wouldn't. His only jewellery appeared to be a wrist watch. No rings. No chains. But he might carry one in his pocket for luck—if he believed in good luck charms, and she doubted that too.

She set the pattern of brilliants into the soft metal with meticulous care, using tiny forceps and a steady hand. When Sally opened the door to ask if she could shut the shop as it was one o'clock Prudence was biting her lower lip with concentration.

'Of course,' she said. 'Be with you in a minute,' and she pressed in a 'star' at the top of a Libran scales.

Sally hesitated, 'Did you mean it, about helping me decorate this afternoon? I mean, you haven't got anything else going?'

'Of course I meant it,' said Prudence.

Everything was spotlessly clean upstairs. It always was. Sally was compulsively neat, there were no fingermarks on *her* walls or doors. But last night she and Lissa had sugar-soaped all the woodwork and moved furniture away from the walls. There were tins of paint and rolls of paper in the middle of the room, and a trestle table and a stepladder on loan from next door.

All Prudence had to do was get cracking, so she tied up her hair in a duster and put on a pink and white gingham check overall, poured emulsion paint into a tray and climbed up the steps carrying the tray and a roller. Sally was painting the bathroom paintwork in eggshell pink—it had been white before. The door was open between the rooms and in the bathroom Sally's cassette recorder played a tape of Barbra Streisand. She was singing 'You don't bring me flowers any more', and Sally was sniffing when they heard the shop door bell ring, and Sally gave a muted shriek.

If Adrian had come back Prudence would hand him her roller and leave them to it, she wasn't decorating for Adrian, and she wasn't expecting him, although Sally was obviously still hoping. Prudence opened the window and looked down. There were fewer cars than usual. Wednesday was early-closing day, but this was one of the main roads and there were still plenty of people around.

She saw the car first, parked just outside the shop, and she had to lean farther out because he was standing with his finger on the doorbell. As she leaned over he looked up. 'Need any help?' he called.

'How are you at ceilings?'

'You've heard of Michaelangelo?'

She laughed, 'This is no Sistine Chapel, but we can use an able-bodied man.'

'Promises, promises!' She wasn't the only one grinning, so were passers-by. She had stepped on a stool to stretch out of the high-up window and Sally had pulled up a chair just behind her and was looking down too. 'Is that Jason Ballinger?' Sally whispered.

'Sure is,' said Prudence. 'Shall we let him in?'

Sally looked at the car, and the man, and said slowly, 'I don't think we could keep him out.'

Prudence went down to open the door. He always generated this feeling of vitality, and as he stepped into the little shop it seemed to Prudence that even the colours of the wools took on a brighter hue. He gave off excitement. He was, heaven knows he was, exceptional.

'Can you take time off whenever you like?' she teased, and he informed her,

'Ah, that's the best about being the boss.'

'I'm the boss here,' she said gaily, 'but I've got to be around.'

They had reached the staircase and he glanced up as he spoke 'How's your assistant?'

'Not so bad,' her voice was low. 'Although she was hoping you were Adrian.'

'No accounting for tastes,' he said, and she told him, laughing,

'I wasn't.'

Sally took the introductions gravely and correctly. She said, 'How do you do,' and offered a drink or a coffee. Jake thanked her and said not just now, and Prudence watched Sally relaxing and starting to giggle as he looked around, at the partly painted ceiling and the two girls in their painting gear, and grinned and asked 'Would you consider the professionals? I could send you one over.'

'A good-looking one?' Prudence joked.

'Built like an all-in-wrestler.'

'That sounds interesting.'

'His wife.'

'Not to bother,' said Prudence. 'Anyhow, we'll finish this by bedtime.' She picked up her tray and roller and Jake said, 'Shall I hold the ladder?'

'I think I might be steadier if you didn't.'

'Would I shake it?' he appealed to Sally, who was giggling now and went on laughing. 'Better let me do it,' he said.

'But have you ever actually painted a ceiling?' asked Prudence, 'I mean, with your own hands.'

'Listen moon lady,' he held out his hands. They

were strong brown hands, and her stomach muscles clenched as though he laid them on her bare skin. 'I've built better places than this with my own hands, from the foundations up.'

'All right, all right!' she laughed. 'Take the roller. Can I offer you a pinafore?'

'You could offer me most things,' he leered, 'but not a pinafore.'

They had an entertaining half hour, during which Jake painted the ceiling of the living room and Prudence helped Sally in the bathroom, while Jake told them about some of the conversions and developments his firm had handled. Prudence wondered how much was literally true, the ghost that walked through one, the subterranean river that nobody knew about until it bubbled up in another. But it all made hilarious telling, and the painting was going well when the phone rang in the office.

Sally froze, paintbrush in hand, the colour ebbing from her cheeks, 'I'll get it,' she said.

'It could be for me,' said Jake, 'I left this number,' but Sally was hurrying downstairs.

'Adrian won't ring her,' said Prudence.

'How do you know?' Jake had put down his paint and roller. He was standing where he could see her through the open door of the bathroom. She was sitting on her heels, painting the skirting board.

'I've seen them,' she said. 'I know the set-up.'

'Have you ever waited for a phone call?' He didn't mean from her father, he meant from a lover, and she said,

'No. Nor you, have you?'

He shook his head, and of course he hadn't. He moved around too much to get involved, and she wondered how long he would remember her when he left here and if he would keep a medallion. She asked, 'Are you Leo or Taurus?'

'What?'

'What's your star sign?'

He didn't believe in that. He looked amused, 'I was born on the twenty-second of November.'

'Oh.' So she hadn't guessed right. 'Scorpio.'

'Is that a fact?'

'Scorpio, the scorpion.' He had walked into the bathroom and was standing looking down at her.

'There's something about you with a duster around your head.' He was smiling, studying her face. He had done that before. He often looked closely at her, but with her hair drawn away from her face she felt very vulnerable. 'You must have been a pretty child,' he said, and she grimaced,

'I don't know why I'm wearing this. I'm not likely to get paint dripping on my head from the skirting board.' She pulled the duster off and shook her dark hair over her face like a veil, as Sally came back into the living room.

'Nobody,' said Sally in answer to Prudence's querying look. 'Well, it was my sister, actually.'

For Sally, for a while, nobody who phoned would count if they weren't Adrian, and Prudence heard herself say sharply, 'She's somebody. Be thankful somebody's phoning you because somebody cares.' She put down her brush, and apologised, 'I seem to be getting snappy. I think I'm hungry.'

They had skipped lunch, planning a takeaway later, but now that Jake was doing so much of the work they could afford to take a break. She said, 'I'll go and get some food.'

Jake didn't offer to accompany her and Sally asked, 'What do I do?' She meant what plates shall we be needing?' Shall I lay the table? She was being thrown into a flutter at the prospect of acting hostess to Jason Ballinger. She couldn't have joked with him like Prudence did.

'You hold the ladder,' said Prudence mischievously, then relented. 'Brew some coffee, and get some plates out. I won't be more than a few minutes.' Sally would be happier busying herself in the kitchenette.

The supermarket was open, and Prudence bought a cooked chicken, and several tubs of assorted salads, some fruit and a crusty loaf. Sally hadn't gone food shopping since Adrian left so that even the bread was stale.

She let herself in by the back door from the parking lot, walking through a small stock room into the shop. Jake was on the phone in the office; she couldn't see him, but she could hear him curtly giving orders to somebody somewhere. He was another man again now, the tycoon was another facet of his character, and probably the main one.

Upstairs Sally had prepared the table down to her silver cruet and linen napkins, which was rather incongruous considering the state of the rest of the room. 'That looks lovely,' Prudence murmured. 'See what I got.' She began to empty her carrier bag and Sally said enthusiastically, 'Oh, I do like him. He's kind, isn't he, he's nice?'

'Isn't he?' said Prudence, thinking, is he? He was clever and charming and tough and a winner all the way, but she suspected there were those who considered that Jason Ballinger was neither nice nor kind.

They ate the meal, sitting at the table, and it was very lighthearted, and sometimes Sally joined in the patter, although most of the time she just listened, smiling. Temporarily, at any rate, she was lifted out of her depression, and afterwards they went on with the decorating.

The paper-hanging benefited from Jake's height and reach. He could hold up the pasted paper while

Prudence and Sally smoothed away the creases beneath; and the room wasn't large. When they had finished it had a new image, and Sally was thrilled. It was dark by then. Jake had taken another couple of phone calls during the afternoon, but apart from that, they had worked undisturbed, and now they stood surveying their efforts and Prudence said, 'I'll bet they haven't made a better job at the Conference Centre.'

'Shall we go and see?' Jake suggested, and smiled at Sally, including her. 'Come on, we'll bring you back.'

'You could stay the night at my place,' Prudence offered. 'The smell of paint in here will give you a headache if you sleep with it.'

'Are you sure?' Sally looked from one to the other and Prudence said, 'Oh, come on!'

Jake walked out with the girls into the car park at the back, seeing them into Prudence's BMW, and as she got behind the wheel he said, 'And don't take your feet off the pedals.'

She grinned, and Sally asked, 'What's he mean?'

'Just a joke,' said Prudence. He was referring to her freewheeling on her bike. They already had private jokes, like friends who had known each other a long time, 'I bet he's easy to work for,' said Sally, and Prudence said nothing, because easy-going was the last thing he was.

Sally had never driven up to the Conference Centre before. She had been to Prudence's home but never to the hotel. She knew it vaguely as an old house a good distance from the road, and now as they followed Jake's car up the wide drive, stopping in front of the flight of steps leading up to the main door, she said, 'It's a big place, isn't it?'

'There's a helicopter pad round the back,' said Prudence. 'And inside it can only be described as palatial.'

'Palatial,' Sally echoed, and nodded, watching Jake go in through the big door, and lights coming on, 'I see what you mean—that is palatial, isn't it?'

Sally was awestruck. And Prudence was impressed at the progress made over the last three days. More painting had been done, paper had been hung in bedrooms, and in the two suites upstairs. The house still echoed, but less than the last time Prudence had walked through, and of course the pool was empty still. The centre would open on schedule unless something catastrophic happened, and nothing would because Jason Ballinger was in control. As they stood by the empty well of the pool, Sally admired the Roman motif on the tiles, Prudence sighed without meaning to. She wished everything wasn't going so well, so fast, but when she caught Jake's eye she laughed and said,

'I'm wishing the water was in.'

'Have patience, Prudence,' he said. 'Are you sure you can swim?'

'She swims very well,' said Sally; and so I should, thought Prudence. There was a swimming pool in our garden when my name was Susie Sinclair. She said, 'I still like the little room with the tower best,' and that was where they ended their tour. The girls sat side by side on the squashy sofa, Jake in a chair, they with glasses of cold wine, he with a whisky, and it was very cosy; and when Prudence said, 'Look at the time, we'd better be going,' it *was* high time, but if Sally hadn't been with her she might have stayed longer. She might have stayed till morning.

When they got home Percy sulked, but Sally expected that, and she really had enjoyed herself this afternoon and this evening. She said she fancied a cup of cocoa for supper, so Prudence made chocolate for two and they sat sipping it and nibbling cheese biscuits, Sally in a cotton nightgown and Prudence in satin pyjamas watching the end of the late-night movie.

It had to be Jake when the phone rang, unless the shop was on fire. Prudence answered with her mouth full of biscuit, 'Hello.'

'Goodnight,' he said. 'I'll see you tomorrow. And you don't need to fill the cottage—Percy's enough.'

She started to laugh, although she hadn't deliberately brought Sally here as chaperone. 'No hassle, I promise,' he said, 'I'll wait to be asked.' She knew that he was smiling too, and she put down the phone smiling, and Sally asked.

'Was it Jake?'

'Yes.'

'I don't think I should be here.'

'That's all right,' said Prudence, telling herself there was always tomorrow.

For the rest of the week Jason Ballinger loomed large in her life. Her dreams were filled with him. In the dark of the night he possessed her with erotic yearnings that made her moan and toss, and almost sent her stumbling downstairs to the phone to ask him to come. But by the time she was fully conscious she realised that waking a man at three with a phone call and the suggestion that he turn out into the cold could be the ultimate turn-off.

He phoned her, but not during the night. They went around together. All her friends and acquaintances knew that Prudence Cormack had met Jason Ballinger and that the rapport had been instant and fierce. Bobby Bygrave asked everyone who tried to discuss the situation with him, who could stand that kind of competition? Ballinger was filthy rich and he had turned Prudence's head. She was a working girl and lord knows what he was promising her.

Jake had promised Prudence nothing, and she wasn't asking for promises. She had never had much faith in them. Right now it seemed that Jake had clicked, which was a silly word, but she felt that their personalities meshed. They laughed at the same things, they talked the same language. She never rang his numbers. In fact she didn't know them, neither at the Conference Centre nor at his offices. But she had the impression that she could call, if she chose, and that he would give her help or advice or anything she needed.

He called her, he fancied her, and very soon she would ask him, with a look or a gesture, or by saying one night, 'Stay.' Very soon. But it was only a week, and although everybody around thought they were sharing a bed, either in her cottage or the Conference Centre, they were not.

This Sunday was very like the last, in that Prudence was one of the hang-gliders on the hill. The weather was right, a little cooler than last week, but the winds were similar and the sun was shining and the hang-gliders gathered.

She had suggested that Jake come along. The evening before they had gone to see a local operatic society do *The Sound of Music*. Prudence had tickets, but she had been surprised when Jake said he would like to go along. The standard was high, but they were amateurs, and she wouldn't have thought *The Sound of Music* was his thing. Anyhow, they went, and it was a good performance and Jake applauded, then afterwards he met some of Prudence's friends and most of the cast, and was charming and complimentary and a hit all round.

'Will you be hang-gliding tomorrow?' one of the hang-gliding club who was playing Captain von Trapp asked Prudence, and she said, 'Very likely,' and asked Jake later, 'How about coming along?'

'I can't,' he said. 'I'm expecting my partner. As soon as you're through how about you coming over to the Centre? We could all go out and eat together.'

She was interested in meeting John Merrick. Jake hadn't said much about him, except that he was an architect and they had known each other for years. During the winter, when the ground became rock-hard or snow-covered, and the air bitterly cold, hang-gliding had to stop, and she would be foolish to waste a few almost perfect hours. Besides, Jake and his partner would have business to discuss. 'Come out and wave when you're ready for me,' she said, 'and I'll be with you in about half an hour.' As she wheeled and hovered high in the sky she watched the smooth lawns of the Centre below.

It was just like last week. She saw the figures, and again she was sure she could pick out Jake. But this time one of the couple with him was a woman, in scarlet with shining blonde hair. She waved when Jake did, but her other hand was through his arm or on his shoulder, they were so close it had to be, and Prudence drew cold air right down into her lungs where it struck sharp, making her wince.

She couldn't get down fast enough. If she had been a bird she would have swooped down in seconds, but she had to use the currents and the wind. Bobby wasn't here today. She could hardly have asked him to fold up her glider and take it home for her if he had been, and this wasn't an emergency that would justify asking anyone else.

She coasted down on the flat top of the hill, and began to unharness herself. Of course there were watchers, just like last week. This time a girl who wanted to know, 'Who's the girl?'

Prudence shrugged. 'I don't know, but I'm going out with them, so I'll probably find out.' She smiled,

and went about packing her glider and hitching it on
to the wheels with her usual unhurried competence.

But she was wasting no time. It suddenly seemed
imperative that she should get across to the Centre as
soon as possible. At home she changed rapidly out of
her gliding outfit into a camel skirt and matching
boots, and a cowl-necked jumper and jacket in purple
mohair. She retouched lips and mascara, then slipped
silver stars in her ears and as always wore her crescent
moon on its thin silver chain.

She walked up the drive to the front door. All the
windows were blank, but soon there would be
curtains, movement, and no longer this feeling of
stillness. She found that she was walking with her
head held high and her shoulders back as though she
was facing an ordeal.

Meeting people didn't worry her. The man was
Jake's partner, the woman someone who knew him
well, and Prudence was here to meet them because
Jake thought they must all have a meal together. Just a
pleasant way of passing an evening. And yet her
mouth was dry and she was torn between wanting to
get there and see what was waiting and a craven urge to
turn and run.

The front door was ajar. Prudence rang the bell,
then pushed the door. The entrance hall, the foyer,
was finished now. The walls were covered with a pale
green-satin sheened paper and the great carved black
marble fireplace was smooth and shining as ebony.
The hall only needed carpeting. It looked like the
entrance to a splendid home, and the girl who stood at
the bottom of the galleried staircase looked at home.

She came forward to meet Prudence like a hostess
greeting a guest, and Jake came with her. He was at
home too, he was the host here, and Prudence blinked
for a second to shut out how right they looked

together. Better than he and I did, she thought, because she's prettier than I am.

Prudence had rarely seen a lovelier girl. She was almost flawless, with her straight small nose, perfect mouth and teeth and huge blue eyes fringed with dark sweeping lashes. Her blonde hair flicked back from her face, and her skin was a pale golden tan that almost certainly went all over. She looked like one of those gorgeous models that advertise expensive cosmetics in glossy magazines. She took your breath away at first sight, so that all Prudence could do was stand there.

Then Jake introduced her, 'This is Tanya and John Merrick,' and Prudence saw the other man. She hadn't noticed him before. All her attention had been centred on Jake and this radiant creature, but now she saw that Tanya had a wedding ring as well as a flashing great diamond on her left hand, and she smiled and said, 'Hello.'

John Merrick was overweight for his height, with a florid complexion and a receding hairline, but he had an attractive smile that made Prudence feel that he was probably a nice man. He looked much older than his wife. Prudence reckoned that if she was out of her teens it was only a matter of months. Her skin was quite smooth there wasn't a blemish or even the hint of a laughter line, although she was smiling too, looking Prudence up and down as though something was amusing her, and Prudence wondered, have I a smudge on my nose or lipstick on my teeth? Am I somehow looking comic, and if I'm not what's the joke?

'It's lovely to meet you,' said Tanya. She had a breathy voice that sounded very young, 'Jake's taste gets better all the time.' She turned to her husband, looking at him from under her lashes and smiling. 'Don't you think so, darling?'

Prudence was obviously the latest in a line of girls that Jake had introduced to the Merricks and on the face of it this was complimentary, but Prudence felt that Tanya was joking at her expense, and she drawled, 'Taste in what?' She was not on inspection. She did not give a damn what John Merrick and his wife thought about her, and if Jake imagined she was here to be compared with his previous conquests she didn't much care what he thought either.

John Merrick ignored both questions and said, 'Jake has been telling us about your suggestion of putting local crafts on sale. It's a good idea.' He indicated a small room leading from the foyer. 'A glass door there,' he suggested, 'and a display cabinet out here, should get them in.'

As long as the terms were reasonable Prudence would be enthusiastic, and she knew several others would jump at the chance. She said, 'Oh yes, what kind of arrangement——?'

'What do you make?' Tanya interrupted. 'I mean, you do make something, don't you?'

'Jewellery,' said Prudence. 'And knitwear.'

'I've just told you that,' said Jake.

'Silly me!' Tanya wrinkled her perfect nose. 'I'm just a goose, completely useless.' She laughed at them all, and she didn't mean a word of it. Her scarlet suit looked Italian, Prudence thought. She would be a status symbol for any man, and her husband was looking at her fondly.

'I'm thrilled with this place,' Tanya told Prudence. 'Jake's been showing us around. I hadn't seen it for a couple of months, isn't it splendid?'

'Yes, indeed,' said Prudence.

'Our home's in London—well, just outside. Hampton Hill. Do you know it?'

'No,' said Prudence.

'Shall we have a drink and a chat and get to know each other?' Prudence couldn't see why Tanya Merrick needed to get to know her. So far they were only booked for a dinner foursome and it wasn't essential to exchange confidences for that. She wondered if Tanya did this to all Jake's girls, and if they were flattered if his partner's wife seemed to like them. She hoped nobody imagined she was here to be vetted.

Tanya put a hand through Prudence's arm and tripped upstairs with her. Tanya wasn't a small girl, she was only a couple of inches shorter than her husband, but she had small hands and she gave an impression of being tiny and dainty. The fingers on Prudence's arm wore a flashing array of rings, and the nails were like pink pearls.

Tanya talked about the layout of the Centre as they went, although this was the third time Prudence had been in here. Of course as her husband had designed it she would be proud of it, and she talked about her husband all the time—John this and John that. Round here they all thought that Jason Ballinger was the big man in Ballinger and Merrick, but Tanya seemed to have no doubt who carried the clout, and she was very much the boss's wife.

She walked into a suite just along the corridor from the room with the tower window. Since Prudence had looked in here on Wednesday it had been furnished and carpeted. A couple of dark blue Persian rugs covered the floor, but the furnishings were modern design. The best of modern design, Prudence felt, almost futuristic. She had seen rooms like this in magazines and Tanya Merrick looked right in here too. Just as she had done in the period setting of the hall. So long as the background was luxurious and expensive she would be at home, Prudence thought, and knew that her attitude was jaundiced because Tanya was patronising her. It made her hackles rise. A smug superior little smile kept lifting the corners of Tanya's mouth when she looked at Prudence. 'Now,' she said, 'what will you have to drink?'

A cupboard on the wall, with dark smoky glass doors, was stocked with three shelves of bottles, and Prudence was about to say stiffly, 'No, thank you.' But that would sound as if she was feeling awkward, so instead she said, 'Sherry please, dry,' and Tanya poured and handed the glass over.

Prudence walked across to the window. The view from here was similar to the tower room, but it didn't have quite such a vista. She couldn't see her chimneys. Tanya seemed to know that she was looking for them. 'Of course, you're the girl with the cottage,' said Tanya. 'Are you selling it to us?'

'I'd rather not. And surely it isn't that important.'

'Well, that was where the garden rooms were on the plan. Of course they can go somewhere else, but Jake likes things his way. I've never known him take no for an answer.'

'There's a first time for everything,' muttered Prudence, and Tanya chortled.

'Not much would be a first for Jason Ballinger. He's a very experienced man. Getting on well with him, are you?'

Prudence wished she hadn't come. In the last week Jake had been her close and exhilarating companion. Not her lover, although both had known that moment was near. His life before she landed at his feet last Sunday hadn't concerned her—any more than Susie Sinclair concerned him—but now she was being treated as a joke, by someone who saw her as another of Jake's girls. Who had seen them all.

She said coolly, 'That depends on what you mean

by getting on,' and Tanya opened her huge blue eyes and shrugged.

'Well, he has one in every port, as they say, and it usually means the same thing. Well, it would, wouldn't it? Don't tell me you're different.'

Prudence decided that she was a mischief-maker—rich and bored and beautiful. You could almost feel sorry for her, except that she had everything and she enjoyed making mischief, so she probably wasn't bored at that.

But Prudence had had enough needling. She was changing the subject. 'Your husband does the designs of the development?' She had already been told he did by Tanya on their way up here, but it might get her talking about John again and off Jake.

'That's right,' said Tanya. 'Jake's the trouble-shooter, John's the artist.' She giggled. 'We make a good team. I'm the sleeping partner.

For a fleeting moment Prudence wondered if that could possibly have a double meaning, and then the two men came in and Tanya turned to her husband, her face alight with laughter, 'I've been trying to warn her about him. I've been telling her. But they take no notice—they won't listen to an old married lady!'

Whether she loves him or not, thought Prudence, she loves being Mrs John Merrick. She wondered if Tanya was John's second wife. As she was so much younger than he, she might well be. She obviously enjoyed having a doting husband, and probably preferred a bachelor partner for him. She was certainly doing nothing to encourage any other girl who might have hopes of joining the team as Mrs Ballinger.

'Oh, but I am different,' said Prudence. 'I always listen to old married ladies.' She laughed, as though she thought it was funny too, but before the men arrived Tanya hadn't been fooling, she had been trying to make Prudence squirm.

Tanya went back to the drinks cupboard, but Jake said, 'No, thanks, I'll be driving.'

'Can't I tempt you?' she smiled into his eyes and Prudence thought wryly. She could tempt a saint, and he's no saint. But he declined again, so Tanya helped John to a drink and herself, then they settled down and discussed the opening of a boutique in the Centre.

A three months' trial was agreed on during which Prudence would have the use of the room, paying a ten per cent commission on sales. Tanya would help in choosing what they were offering, and Prudence was not too happy about that. She had no doubt that Tanya had taste but that she would be more likely to be bossy than helpful, and when Tanya said, 'I could act as consultant, couldn't I?' Prudence said,

'I wouldn't be bringing anything here that I wouldn't offer in my own shop. So if there's something that I think is good and saleable, but you disagree, who has the final word?'

'I do,' said Jake.

'Fine by me,' said Prudence. He was too successful a businessman to let personalities influence him.

'But of course,' said Tanya, clapping her hands as though this was a game that was going to be fun. Prudence would have preferred to be left to her own devices and judged on results, but she was landed with Tanya.

The evening was not all that wonderful, although around seven o'clock they drove out to a luxury hotel and ate a fabulous meal. Tanya talked most, in her breathy little-girl voice, usually about people whom Prudence had never met.

But she could imagine them. She amused herself doing that as Tanya trilled on and looked up from her plate one time to meet Jake's ironic glance as if he appreciated how boring this was for her. When he smiled she smiled back, and Tanya, who had been talking about an exhibition of furniture by a designer whose name meant nothing to Prudence, reached to touch Jake's arm and said, 'By the way, Gilda was there and she asked me to tell you she's bought the most exciting new bed—Swedish. She said it's an incredible experience. She seemed to think you might be interested.'

She laughed, and Jake said, 'The mind boggles,' and Prudence could imagine Gilda, but not her bed. Her mind closed on that, and she was swelteringly hot in her mohair and wondering how soon she could start stifling yawns and hope that one of the men would take the hint and suggest they headed home.

But after the meal there was dancing on the small highly polished floor. Prudence danced with Jake, and when she felt his arms around her her knees went weak. He held her close, his cheeks against hers. 'What do you think of John?' he asked. John and Tanya were sitting with their heads together, their eyes following Jake and Prudence as though they were discussing them.

'He seems very pleasant,' said Prudence. Then she added, 'But I don't know about her. Does she always carry on like this?'

'Only if there's another woman around with what it takes to take the limelight off her.'

'You don't mean me?'

'Of course I mean you.'

'You say the nicest things,' she said. 'No wonder you've got a girl in every port!'

'Who says?'

'Guess who?'

It was nearing midnight by then. To late to start

telling herself that Tanya's attitude was ridiculous rather than riling. It was absurd that so beautiful a girl could resent other women, but obviously it could happen. Her husband seemed to find her endearing. He was besotted with her, you could see that. And perhaps she thought all men should be. Including Jake.

Prudence hoped she didn't have to see much of her. She would deal with the problems of the boutique as they turned up, and Tanya probably had a low boredom threshold. Prudence couldn't imagine her getting involved in real work for long, but she would be around for a while. The Merricks were taking over that private suite at least until the Centre was opened and running smoothly. On and off they would be living there, and Prudence wasn't particularly thrilled about that. Nobody was asking Prudence's opinion, of course, it just came up in the conversation. Like the news that Jake was flying to France in the morning and would be away until the weekend. Altogether Prudence had not enjoyed her evening with the Merricks, although when she said her goodbyes she assured them all that it had been delightful.

She asked to get out of the car when they reached her cottage, and Jake drew up and she jumped out quickly. 'I'll see you next Saturday,' he said.

'I'll be here, unless I get a better offer.'

She was being deliberately flippant. If she hadn't just been reminded that there had been girls for Jake before her, and there would be others after her, she would have been ready to ask him to stay with her tonight. But having that spelled out had made her wary again. And now there was nearly a week to decide if she wanted her name on his list.

Tonight was the first she had heard about him going away, although he jetted on business all over the world. Perhaps he hadn't mentioned it before because he hadn't known about it. It might have come out of the talk he had had with John Merrick. Perhaps Jake was being given the orders for a change. She would see how much she missed him. When they met again next Saturday she would know if the game was worth the candle.

She had been sitting in the back of the car with Tanya, in the off-seat, and she had scrambled out into the road. As she came round the car she found herself facing Jake, who had got out of the driving seat, and who put his hands on her shoulders and pulled her towards him and kissed her hard. His grip on her shoulders was hard, and when he loosed her she looked up into his hard inscrutable face; then he smiled. 'Any offers you get,' he said, 'I'll make you a better.'

Prudence stood there as the car drew away, a clenched fist pressed to her mouth. She wasn't smiling because she was watching Tanya's face through the back window, and Tanya was shaking with a laughter that Prudence was almost sure was silent.

CHAPTER FIVE

PRUDENCE was surprised how much she missed Jake, although she should have expected it, because he had monopolised her spare time. Since she met him they had spent every evening together and the evenings this week lacked something without him. She didn't sit around. She had plenty of other friends, some who were very dear to her, but no matter what company she was in she missed Jake.

Even at Meon Farm. On Tuesday, after work, she took a white lacy shawl over to Jean's. She usually took a baby gift these days, the baby was due in a few weeks. She and Jean sat in Jean's comfortable living room and chattered away. Jean wanted the latest news about Jake and Prudence explained that he was abroad this week, and told her the plans for the boutique at the Centre.

Jean listened to the business talk, but when Prudence paused she asked, 'Is it getting serious?'

'What? Oh,' Prudence laughed, 'you're still on about Jake. No, of course it isn't serious.'

It was not, and never would be, a serious relationship, but she missed him. She had become a little dependent on him, and when he left for good she would miss him more than a little. It was Tuesday night and he would be back on Saturday, and she was counting the days. More than that, she was starting to count the hours.

She hoped nobody guessed. If anyone did it would be Tanya Merrick, who arrived at the shop on Wednesday morning, wearing a full-length snow lynx coat and grey suede boots, having stepped out of a silver Daimler that had drawn up outside, halting the traffic.

It was cold today. The women in the high street were in thick coats, but not many of them had seen a coat like Tanya's before, and most of them were convinced she had to be a TV star at least. When she walked into the shop a hush fell in there too. Three customers looked at her, and then at each other, eyebrows raised as Tanya's glance swept over them and settled on Sally.

Prudence was in her workroom when Sally rushed in to say she was wanted. 'Who is it?' Prudence enquired, but Sally hadn't stopped to ask the name.

'I don't know, but she's sensational.'

'That sounds like Tanya,' said Prudence.

They had been expecting her. On Sunday night she had told Prudence she would be calling round some time, although she couldn't say when. 'She's the wife of Jason Ballinger's partner?' Sally had recapped when Prudence reported Sunday's decisions to her on Monday morning, and Prudence put it bluntly.

'She's the boss's wife. John Merrick seems to be the senior partner. Tanya Merrick is giving us the benefit of her advice and I can't see her letting us forget that we're the peasants. I think she'll crack the whip.'

That had Sally worried, and Prudence had wished she'd been less outspoken, but on the other hand she felt Sally should be warned that they would be dealing with a spoiled little bitch. Prudence was finding it hard to forget the sight of Tanya laughing, as though Jake kissing Prudence goodbye was such a joke . . .

When the two girls walked into the shop Tanya was standing in front of one of the wall-case jewellery displays, and she turned to greet them with a dazzling smile. Her eyes sparkled and her small perfect teeth gleamed between coral lips. 'These are very attractive,' she said.

Prudence was taken aback, she had expected Tanya to start carping right away. 'Thank you,' she said.

'And sensibly priced,' Tanya went on smoothly. 'I'm sure we're going to do well with these.' Sally was moving away, towards the customers, and Tanya looked straight into Prudence's face and dropped her voice slightly to ask, 'Have you heard from Jake?'

Prudence was suddenly sure that Tanya was here to tell her he would not be returning on Saturday, and the disappointment was bitter. She felt as though she was crumpling inside, fighting to keep it from showing in her face. 'No,' she said through dry lips. 'Is anything the matter?'

'Of course not.' Perhaps Prudence had betrayed herself, because Tanya sounded amused. 'How could it be, with Jake there? John has the greatest confidence in him. He's John's right-hand man. No, I just wondered if he'd phoned.'

'Not me,' said Prudence brightly. 'Well, not yet.'

Sally was reassured about Tanya well before they closed the shop for half-day. Tanya took off her coat, under it she wore a soft grey dress with a lace Peter Pan collar that made her look like an exquisite schoolgirl, and she went through the stock and round the shop, admiring everything.

She didn't patronise Sally, the way she had tried to put Prudence down. Instead she chatted, girl to girl; and with Prudence. As though they were all in a venture together and the last thing in her mind was pulling rank.

Prudence could hardly believe her eyes, but she was glad there had been a change and when Tanya suggested the three of them went along to the Centre this afternoon, to take a look at the room that would be the shop, Prudence said yes, of course. She would bet her life there would be problems. Some time, somehow, Mrs Tanya Merrick would rock the boat, but Prudence was all for accomplishing as much as possible while her mood was sunny.

Sally thought she was lovely. When Sally went to get her coat Prudence went up to the flat too, and Sally said, 'She doesn't seem a bit snobby. I thought she'd be awful.'

'So did I,' said Prudence. 'Perhaps she was having an off-day on Sunday.'

At the Centre Tanya continued to be one of the girls. Workmen were around. Prudence had never been inside the house before during working hours and it seemed a hive of activity compared with how it felt when it was empty and echoing.

The little room off the foyer had been painted with white walls and fitted with shelves and assigned as a spare storeroom-cum-office. But it would make a super little shop and Prudence knew she was getting a good deal. With no overheads they couldn't lose, and Sally said, 'Well, I think it's wonderful. Thank you very much, Mrs Merrick.'

'Please,' Tanya persisted, 'Tanya. I thought we were on first-name terms—you haven't been thinking of me as Mrs Merrick, have you? Anyhow, I'm not the one you should thank. We've had sales counters before but not entirely local goods, and when Jake asked my husband on Sunday John said yes, give it a go. So,' she smiled looking around the little room with them, 'here we are and it's John you have to thank. Now, wallpaper, I think, don't you?'

Afterwards she took them up to her suite, and Sally went into raptures over that. 'John and I often move into the latest development for a little while,' said Tanya. 'I suppose it appeals to the gypsy in me—I do love change, excitement.'

Jake had said he had no settled home, he always moved around. Two restless people, thought Prudence; and Tanya went into the bedroom and came out holding a photograph. It was John Merrick before his hair started to recede. He looked younger, almost handsome. 'This is my husband.' Tanya showed Sally, who sighed,

'Oh, you are lucky!' Prudence knew she was thinking about Adrian, and was glad about the shop downstairs because it would be a fresh interest. Sally could come over here and meet new people and get out of the rut and maybe stop brooding.

'I know I'm lucky,' said Tanya smugly. 'He's a wonderful husband—so generous. He thinks the world of me.'

The open bedroom door showed a room furnished like this room, in entirely modern style. There were twin beds, with leopardskin covers, and on one an open suitcase. 'Are you going or coming?' Prudence heard herself ask.

'Right now,' said Tanya, 'going. Until Sunday, maybe.'

'Anywhere interesting?' asked Prudence.

'Very,' Tanya smiled. 'Well, people make places, don't they? If you're with someone who's exciting you're not going to get bored.'

'You mean your husband?' Sally said wistfully, still looking at the photograph of the man with the kind face who was generous, and Tanya took it from her and put it back on the table by the bed. 'Of course,' she said.

As Prudence drove Sally to her flat Sally raved about Tanya. She couldn't get over Prudence thinking she was standoffish. John Merrick was obviously the big name in the firm, but Tanya, said Sally, was sweet.

Prudence kept her eyes on the road and said nothing. She was driving very carefully this evening. One of the painters and decorators at the Centre had asked her, 'Do you drive a white B.M.W. through Eyesford most mornings?' and when Prudence said she did he said, 'I thought I recognised you. I watch out for you. You nearly got me head-on a couple of weeks back.'

She had apologised and said she remembered and that it was her fault, she had skidded. He had grunted at that as though he suspected she often used the wrong side of the road, and he would go on watching for her car as long as this job meant he was likely to be passing her each morning.

She had been thinking about Jake then. She had only just met him, but he had obsessed her thoughts so that she had nearly crashed into that poor man.

By her side Sally went on talking about Tanya Merrick's perfect marriage, and about Tanya and how helpful she was being. They had chosen a daisy-patterned wallpaper that looked fresh and young, all three girls agreeing on it; and when Prudence suggested that some of the jewellery could be unisex and some of the knitwear, Tanya had said enthusiastically, 'What a good idea.' It had all been friendly, Tanya couldn't have been nicer, and Sally said now, 'Isn't she beautiful? And so happy. Oh, I'm sure she isn't going to cause us any trouble.'

'I hope not,' Prudence murmured. Today Tanya had been sweet as honey, as if she was entirely satisfied with the way things were going. Prudence couldn't believe that was just the boutique and she wondered what else could be pleasing Tanya so much . . .

Jake did phone next day. On Thursday afternoon he rang Prudence at the shop. She answered the phone and her heart gave a skip at the sound of his voice.

'Hello,' she said, 'and please don't tell me you won't be back on Saturday.'

'What gave you that idea?'

'I'm psychic.' She said it laughing, but she was scared that something might happen to keep him away.

'No, you're not,' he said. 'I'll see you around seven.'

This time her heart skipped with pleasure. 'I didn't get a better offer,' she said. 'I'll be waiting. What shall we do?'

'There's a question.' Sally was watching her, as she sat on the side of the desk cradling the receiver against her glowing cheek, laughing and talking softly.

'I mean, how shall I dress?'

'Why bother?'

'Because it's very cold here.'

'Now I do have some ideas about that.'

They talked on a little while longer and when Prudence put down the phone she started to say, 'That was——'

'I know,' said Sally.

Now I can get through the rest of the week, thought Prudence. She had got through up to now very well, doing everything she ought to do as efficiently as always. She hadn't wasted her time or gone off her food, but now that it was certain that Jake would be knocking on her door at seven o'clock on Saturday night she felt much happier. She *had* missed him. She wanted to hear what he had been doing. She wanted to tell him about her week. Nothing remarkable had happened to her, but she could spin out a few things to make him smile. Meeting the man who had been driving that car, for instance, and being told he still held his breath every morning when he saw her on the horizon.

The next time she spoke to Jake on the phone he

was back in the Centre. It was Saturday evening, and
he said, 'You've got half an hour.'

'That'll do me,' she said.

'Everything all right?'

'Couldn't be better.' He could have come for her
then, she was ready. She had hurried from the
moment she got home, singing most of the time
because she was in such high spirits. She knew that
she looked good, and that it was partly because she felt
so good, and while she waited for seven o'clock she
curled up in a chair and took her first look at the
morning paper. Sometimes this arrived before she left
for work, usually after. Today it had been waiting on
the hall floor when she got back, and now she had a
few minutes to spare she began to scan the headlines
and turn the pages.

There was a photograph on page four that hit her
like a blow. She sat, staring at it, the colour draining
from her cheeks. The same photograph had stood on
her mother's dressing table, of a smiling man and a
child of eight or nine, with her arms around his neck.

No one would recognise Prudence as the child, she
had changed so much, and she would never know now
how the years had changed her father, because he was
dead. His car had crashed on a mountain pass in Spain
earlier in the week. He had a villa, another name, he
had been living there for years in comfortable
circumstances, but this among his papers had
identified him as the missing embezzler David
Sinclair.

He had kept her photograph—God knows why,
considering what he had done to her and to his wife,
and Prudence felt no deep grief, how could she? but
there was some sorrow. She had loved him, a long
time ago, and depression descended on her now. She
put down the newspaper and sat with her hands lying

loosely in her lap. She didn't even have the cat for comfort, he had trotted out a few minutes earlier, and when Jake knocked on the door she stood up and shook herself impatiently as though she could throw off her melancholy mood.

She greeted him with a smile, 'Hello, it's good to see you,' and he asked without any hesitation, 'What's the matter?'

She couldn't be hiding it too well. Her smile vanished, and she had to bite her lip and admit, 'I've just had rather a shock. I've just heard that somebody's died. We knew him a long time ago, but he wasn't all that old.'

'Someone close to you?'

'Oh, *no*. No.' There had been an unbridgeable distance between them. She began to cover up, inventing. Nobody would blame her, at this stage, for being David Sinclair's daughter, but she wanted no part of that name ever again. So she talked about a retired bank manager in Edinburgh and a phone call she had just had from someone who had mentioned that he had died. Then she said, 'And that's enough about that. Now, how are you? How's life? How's business?'

'Couldn't be better,' said Jake, 'on all counts.' Prudence looked around for her coat, although she had intended to suggest they might stay. She could have rustled up a meal. But now she wanted to get out of here and away from that newspaper. When she came back she would burn it. It would never be connected with her, but she wanted to get rid of it, and he wasn't expecting to spend the evening in her cottage, he was waiting for her.

Her camel coat was warm and enveloping, with a big collar, and as she struggled to get her arms into the sleeves he helped her on with it, pulling up her collar and kissing the tip of her nose, and she thought how lovely it would be to be taken care of. She could take care of herself, she had had enough practice, but his hands wrapping her coat cosily around her, and the kiss that tickled her nose and made her want to sneeze and smile, seemed cherishing, and she thought, I would like to be cherished. I would like him to care for me so much that I could tell him anything.

'Where are we going?' she asked.

'There's something I want to show you at the Centre.'

'Is the shop papered?' There was plenty of time for that, but she was looking forward to seeing the little room prettied up.

'Wait and see,' he said.

They met Percy as they came out of the house and Prudence said, 'I've left your supper in the kitchen, you go in and stay by the fire, I won't be late home.'

'Don't bank on that, buster,' said Jake.

It was cold for early November. There was frost in the air and a silver shimmer on the trees and grass. They walked up the drive with his arm round her, the way they usually seemed to walk, and she thought, it's going to be a hard winter, but he and Tanya can follow the sun.

They weren't talking, but she bit her lip as though she had just said the wrong words. She didn't want Jake and Tanya linked together, not even in her thoughts.

The only lights on in the Centre were in the hall. When Jake opened the door it was shadowy in the gallery at the top of the staircase, but as Prudence looked up she half expected to see the pale glimmer of Tanya's face and the bright glint of her hair. 'Anybody else at home?' she asked on just the right casual note, and when he said, 'No,' she was glad. She would like this tour of inspection to end in the room with the tower window.

She was feeling numb. It was the cold of the walk up here and of course the shock of that newspaper story. But being with Jake was helping, if anyone could take her mind off her secret sadness he could, and the door to the boutique had been removed and the wall just inside was daisy-covered.

She hurried across with a cry of delight. She needed to get her enthusiasm going. 'It *was* pretty. She was going to be thrilled about it. She said, 'Yes, oh *yes!*' and turned, smiling, but most of her gaiety was acting.

'Seems to be coming on all right.' Jake switched on the light and the room was only half finished, but you could see how it would be. 'Who chose the paper?'

'We all did. Tanya brought Sally and me up here on Wednesday and we all chose it. She was very charming.' Tanya had been charming. She had woven a gay girlish spell that had made an instant fan of Sally.

'Good,' said Jake. He moved away from the doorway, and Prudence got the impression that he didn't want to talk about Tanya, but she asked idly, 'How long have they been married?'

'John and Tanya? Oh, about seven years.'

That startled her. 'I've heard of child brides—she can't be more than twenty now!'

'She's twenty-seven.' Three years older than Prudence was.

'I thought—well, she looks about nineteen.'

He smiled, 'She wears well.'

An utterly unlined skin at twenty-seven wasn't luck so much as dedication. A lot of time devoted to keeping herself beautiful.

'She wears beautifully,' said Prudence.

'Now,' said Jake, 'come and tell me what you think about this.'

He took her hand and led her along the corridor to the sports area. They passed the squash courts and the gymnasium and went through the doors to the swimming pool. 'Stand still,' he said. She saw the water shining in the pool, but it looked dark and deep and sinister until he began turning on lights when, suddenly, it was sparkling clean. Turquoise tiles under water, and lights like sunshine overhead, made it as inviting as a South Seas picture postcard. The jacuzzi bubbled and the surface of the pool was smooth as glass.

It was like watching the Christmas lights go on, and this time her surprised delight was genuine. She clapped her hands. 'There's water in the pool!' and Jake said,

'That's what it is, water.'

She went down on her knees to dip her fingers in the steaming jacuzzi. 'Oh, it's beautifully hot! Who'll be using it, between now and the opening?'

The men who were working here. He would. The Merricks would. It would be used. 'But,' he said, 'I think you should be first.'

She laughed, 'Don't tell me nobody's swum here yet?'

'Not officially. Do you swim?'

'What if I don't?'

'I'll teach you.'

'I might have enjoyed that.' This had lifted her depression. This would wash the sadness away. 'I don't have a swimsuit,' she said. 'You should have told me.'

'Do you need one?' She had a good body, but she was not stripping starkers for a dip where somebody doing overtime could stroll in.

'Yes, I do,' she said. 'So I'll fetch one.'

'Don't worry, I brought you one back.'

She didn't know what was coming, and when he picked up a candy-striped carrier bag with a French name scrawled across it, from one of the lounger chairs, she raised an eyebrow and asked, 'How did you know my size?'

'Silly question.'

'I'm a cover-up girl,' she warned, exaggerating but playing safe, and she took out a one-piece swimsuit in brilliant pink and said, 'Thank you,' in pleased surprise.

'What were you expecting?'

She liked this very much, she would get a lot of pleasure out of it, and she laughed, 'I thought perhaps a very brief bikini.'

'No,' he said. 'All or nothing, that's you.'

That was not what Bobby would say. Nobody around had thought Prudence was capable of wild extremes. 'And you're expecting me to jump in the deep end tonight?' she said, brows arched, lips curved.

'I wouldn't let you sink.'

She didn't believe he would. She believed he would catch her if she jumped. And she laughed and went to the changing rooms carrying her pink suit.

There were two changing rooms, the smaller for women because most of those who attended conferences here would be men. One wall was one huge mirror, and as she undressed Prudence thought, I could have changed by the pool. There were only the two of us, it shouldn't have bothered me, so why did I hurry into here?

Perhaps she was still holding back, preserving a little reticence. Perhaps they had not yet reached the moment of naked truth. She looked at her reflection; the suit was slashed high, emphasising her leggy grace, and shaped smooth and taut over her breasts. It was only a silken handful, but it was a barrier, and Tanya came into her mind again. Tanya's reflection would appear on this wall much more frequently than Prudence's, and as late as this she felt that Tanya would swim naked, golden all over.

She slipped down the straps from her own shoulders, then grimaced faintly because she wasn't golden-skinned, she was moon-pale, and besides, somebody else *could* turn up. She hitched the straps back into place and bent down to shake her hair forward, up from her neck, then twisted it high in a topknot. Tendrils fell around her face, but it would keep her hair out of her eyes while she was swimming.

Jake was sitting by the pool, wearing brief black trunks, back, chest, arms, legs, tanned so dark that he could have been a bronze statue. Then he saw her and smiled and the statue came to life.

'Well, go on,' she said. 'Jump in.'

'After you.'

The water was smooth. Not a ripple broke the surface. Prudence said, 'I declare this pool open,' and dived from the side with hardly a splash. It felt like cool silk, streaming past her in a glittering blue world, and when she came up for air Jake was swimming beside her. 'I like your hairstyle,' he said.

It was dripping wet and no style at all, and she smiled, 'I like your pool.'

'Consider it yours.'

The nearest public baths were ten miles away. This, on her doorstep, would be bliss, and so beautifully warm. She began to play, swimming fast, swimming slow, running through her repertoire of strokes. Not showing off, just enjoying herself. Jake couldn't have taken her anywhere tonight that would have been more fun or more relaxing.

'You're a pretty swimmer,' he commented, as she drifted along in a leisurely back-stroke.

'I am, aren't I? Oh, this is *lovely*!'

It was a super pool, she would have enjoyed a swim in it any time, but tonight there had been the excitement of surprise, and there being just the two of them gave it a special magic. She swam into Jake's arms more than once and he kissed her cool skin with cool lips, and they floated together and drifted apart like dancers. Sometimes they caught hands or hooked a finger, sometimes she was against the whole length of him and he wrapped his arms around her and they went down smiling at each other, then bobbed up again, laughing and blinking the water out of their eyes. They swam, and fooled, and it was fabulous. They must have been in the water for ages when Prudence, treading water at the deep end, asked, 'What's the time?'

'You may have noticed,' said Jake, 'I'm not wearing a watch. Are you flagging?'

She was suddenly less buoyant. She swam back a little slower and said, 'I think I'll try the jacuzzi.'

After the pool the bubbling water felt boiling. She yelped when she stepped into it, and sat on the side dipping her feet in and out. Jake settled down on a lower step, a contented grin on his face.

'You must have a hide like a rhinoceros,' she said.

'Charming!'

'This is scalding me.'

'You'll be surprised how soon you acclimatise.'

He was right. She slithered down as her body heat adjusted, and the bombardment of bubbles became a pleasurable sensation, like having an underwater massage, or being tickled gently. But she still kept clear from the waist up, because she was feeling exhausted and she didn't want the heat to go to her head.

She asked, 'What was it like in France?'

'Dull but profitable. What have you been doing?'

Nothing that amounted to much. The boutique opening here was the only change in her life. She told him that Sally was still depressed and when they opened she thought it might do her good to come up here and see some new faces.

'Sure,' he said. 'Any sign of the bloke you hit over the head?'

'Adrian? He hasn't contacted Sally, but he's about. I didn't damage him permanently.'

Jake chuckled at that, and she remembered that she had to tell him she had met the man who worked for him, who now watched out for her every morning in case she skidded his way again. But that story wasn't funny any more, because earlier this week that was how her father had been killed.

Something had happened to Prudence since she last saw Jake. She had lost the father whose face she could hardly recall. 'My father has died,' she could have said. She stepped out of the jacuzzi, her breath catching as the pool struck chill, 'Race you three lengths!' she called, and pushed herself away in a racing crawl.

She was conscious of Jake close behind her and knew he could have passed her and remembered her father letting her win in the pool at home. She had believed she was faster, but of course she wasn't. He had been kind to her then, she had loved him then, and she wished she had never known when he died because it was dreadful that she couldn't weep for him.

The numbness inside her was back again. She had shut off those early years, never letting herself dwell on them, and now they seemed like a dream with no reality. She could not remember her father's face, although she had just seen it again in that photograph, and she had remembered the photograph.

She turned for the third length, and this time Jake went ahead and hauled himself out so that he could take her wrists when she reached for the side and lift her out of the water. She was lightheaded. She had swum too fast. A man had died on Tuesday, but he had not been Prudence Cormack's father. Prudence Cormack had no roots, and if the past wasn't real how could she be sure of the present? Maybe all her friends were shadows, and her cottage and her shop, and there was nothing anywhere that would endure. She put her hands flat on Jake's chest and it was solid as a rock; he was no shadow. She could feel his slow steady heartbeats against her cold fingertips, and she was asking to be kept alive when she whispered huskily, 'Hold me, please. Please, oh, please, *love me!*'

He wrapped her in a huge fluffy white towel, she must have started shivering, and he carried her. He was strong, she wouldn't have thought she was light enough to carry so easily so far. She closed her eyes and turned her head so that her cheek lay against his shoulder. She might tell him about her father, but she couldn't put it into words yet, and like a tired child she gave herself up to the comfort of being carried. She knew when they climbed the stairs, she knew the turns in the corridor, and when they reached his room she slid to her feet, opening her eyes although her lids were heavy. She leaned against him as he opened the door, and he picked her up again to carry her in, across the living room into the bedroom. She hadn't seen this room before, she hadn't been in here. She didn't see it now, only the pale shape that was the window, as he laid her on the bed.

He slipped the wet swimsuit from her shoulders, peeling it off, drying her gently with a towel; and then she was between the sheets and he was undoing the knot of her hair. It was wet and clammy and he rubbed it for a few moments, and Prudence couldn't remember when her hair was last towelled dry. It was still damp when he lay down beside her and started to make love to her.

He was an expert. He knew so well how to arouse a woman's physical needs, and he would know how to satisfy them. From the firm resilience of his flesh warmth was flowing into her, and she responded with increasing ardour, moving her body in sensuous joy at being alive, at being made to feel so good. This was natural and healing, and she was melting and clinging because this was going to be the loveliest lovemaking that had ever happened to her.

She would remember it all. But then it changed, and she wasn't melting she was burning. His touch and his kisses and his closeness were wrapping her in liquid fire. She had never known there could be such pleasure, and such exquisite pain that she never wanted to stop. She had no clear idea any longer what she was doing, or what was being done to her, except that she was flying higher than she had ever flown, and at the crescendo of it all she seemed to explode in a million stars as though she had gone up like a meteorite . . .

'Coffee,' said Jake. She usually woke at the slightest sound, but this morning she couldn't open her eyes. She must have been in a deep, deep sleep, for Jake's voice not to stir her. Then he touched her shoulder and she felt that and her eyes flew open. 'Coffee.'

'Thanks.' The room was very light. She struggled to sit up in bed and take the coffee cup. The sheet fell away from her bare shoulders and she gasped, then shrugged, because what were bare shoulders after last night?

Jake was dressed and shaved, wearing slacks and an

oatmeal polo-neck and barefooted. 'What do you eat for breakfast?' he asked.

'Not a lot,' she said, 'and I think I'd better go home for it.'

'Why?' There was no rush. She had nothing planned for today and Percy could wait for his breakfast.

'Just coffee, then,' she said, 'unless you can run to toast.'

She wished he would sit on the bed and put an arm around her. She didn't expect him to get back into bed again. It was morning and he probably had work to do and it was high time she was out of his bed, but last night had been so incredible that it surely rated a good-morning kiss.

Looking back, she could hardly believe that she had lost her head so completely. She had never realised she was capable of such consuming passion. Her lip stung when she sipped her coffee and she looked across at Jake and wondered if, under that sweater, he was marked. If she had raked him with her nails or left teeth marks on his shoulder. I don't know, she thought, but I'm beginning to believe I was capable of anything. I remember thinking he was devouring me.

'Toast coming up,' he said, 'and that door's the bathroom.'

She turned her head to look at the door. 'Do you have a spare robe or shirt or something? I left everything downstairs.'

'Help yourself,' he said.

Nothing had changed. He was glad she was here. There was a good sexy rapport between them, but last night had not been mind-blowing for him. It had been enjoyable and lusty, and he had got up this morning and showered and shaved and dressed because—like Tanya said—he was a man of very wide experience, so

this morning was no different for him from countless
other mornings.

Prudence waited for him to leave the bedroom
before she climbed out of bed and went into the
bathroom, and when she looked at her reflection in the
mirror she winced. Her eyes were bleary and her hair
was dull as seaweed, and she got under the shower,
letting the water run through her hair and down her
body, keeping it cool enough to shock her awake.

She didn't have any bruises. She craned her neck,
looking at herself from all angles, and thought wryly—
That's the mark of the expert, no marks. She
shouldn't have expected Jake Ballinger to have
changed this morning because they had been on a ride
to the stars together. He had gone along with her, but
she was the one who had never known anything like it
before, and although it had been wonderful, fantastic,
she would not be doing it again in a hurry.

He had made her feel too much, the loving had been
so fierce it had been frightening. She would remember
it for a long time, but she would think twice before she
begged him to help her through another night.

The robe behind the door would have tripped her
up if she had tried to walk in it, and it seemed stupid
to borrow a shirt for a few minutes while she ran down
to the changing rooms to get her own clothes, so she
wrapped a towel around her, tucking it in securely. It
might be chilly in the rest of the house and she didn't
even have any shoes.

She was nearly at the door into the corridor when
someone knocked and she hesitated. She thought it was
John Merrick's voice that called, 'Jake, are you in?'

'Yes,' she called back, she was adding, 'Well,
somewhere,' when the door opened and it was
Merrick. He looked astonished, then embarrassed,
then he began to apologise.

'I'm sorry . . .'

'Jake is around.' Prudence wished she was sophisticated enough to carry off a situation like this without blushing to the roots of her hair. 'Tanya with you?' she asked, for something to say.

'No,' he said. 'I came down a little earlier than I planned, but she doesn't seem to be around.'

She heard Jake coming. He had her clothes over his arm and he was carrying her shoes. 'Hello,' he said, when he saw John.

'I've lost Tanya,' said John. He grinned and so did Jake, but Prudence thought the smiles were strained. 'She should be here, but she doesn't seem to be. That room wasn't used last night.'

'Can't help you, I'm afraid,' said Jake. 'I got back after the workmen had gone and there was no one here then. She knows you're coming today, does she? Then she'll be along.'

'Of course,' said John Merrick. He smiled at Prudence. 'Sorry,' he said again. 'Excuse me.'

'What was that all about?' asked Prudence.

'Crossed wires,' said Jake. 'He thought she was here and she wasn't, but she will be by this afternoon. She spends half her time at health farms and beauty clinics and nobody's supposed to know about it. John does, of course, but I suppose he feels the result's worth the money.'

'There's an alibi,' Prudence muttered.

'What?'

'Well, I hope she is at a health farm. She was packing on Wednesday when Sally and I were here and she said she was going somewhere with someone exciting. Sally said did she mean her husband and she said, "Of course".' She stopped, and Jake said harshly,

'Forget it. If John buys the health spa that's what he wants to believe and that's how we leave it.'

Jake had suspicions about Tanya, that was obvious. And so had her husband, and that was sad. 'It's no business of mine,' said Prudence. 'I don't know where she's been and I don't much care.'

She picked up her clothes from a chair and went into the bathroom with them. She wanted to get dressed. She didn't want to wander around here any longer with nothing but a towel tucked round her.

CHAPTER SIX

I COULD use some make-up, Prudence thought. She had a purse with a lipstick, still downstairs in the changing room, but up here she looked wan and wet, her hair dark and shining from the shower. She rubbed it a little, and remembered the feel of Jake's fingers in her hair, and put the towel back on the rail. She wasn't blushing now. She had coloured scarlet when John Merrick came into the room and found her here, but the blood had drained from her face as quickly as it had flared. Now she was pale again and it wouldn't have taken much to have started her shivering. She dressed completely before she came out of the bathroom, even to shoes.

She wasn't wearing her moon charm. She couldn't remember taking it off, but the fragile chain could easily have broken during the night, it would have been a wonder if it hadn't, and she wanted it because she always wore it and she liked it and maybe it was lucky.

She hoped Jake wouldn't be in the bedroom if she had to start taking the bed apart and searching between the sheets, but a cleaning staff had been recruited from the village and somebody local would be making that bed, and if they discovered Prudence Cormack's moon charm that would provide a lovely bit of scandal, so it had to be found.

As she came out of the bathroom she saw the silver necklet on the table by the bed. The chain wasn't broken. Jake must have slipped it over her head when he was peeling off her wet swimsuit, and there were a couple of silver rings. She remembered the swimsuit, but nothing else. She had pierced ears, her earrings were tiny stars. She touched, checking, and she was still wearing them. I wasn't quite naked, she thought crazily. Out of my mind, but still wearing my earrings.

She put the chain round her neck again and slipped her fingers into her rings, then went towards the closed door leading to the room with the tower window. She could hear someone moving around. That would be Jake, and when she walked through it would be nice if he looked as dazed as she felt. As though this morning had broken like the first morning.

There was a tray, with toast and a butter dish and a pot of some conserve and a coffee pot, on a small low table. Jake was standing by the window, drinking coffee. The light behind him caught the red glints in his hair and emphasised the dark tan of his skin. 'How's the weather look?' she asked, peering past him at the sky because it wasn't easy to stare straight at him. Not if she was going to stay calm.

Now he *was* cool. Of course he was. Last night had been no blinding revelation for him. He had heard the weather forecast while he was down in the kitchens, filling this tray, and the forecast was squally, not hang-gliding weather.

'Pity,' she said. She sat down beside the little table and poured herself another cup of coffee. She was pleased to see that her hands were fairly steady. 'See,' she could have said, 'that's all the practice I've had making my jewellery. My hands don't shake no matter how I'm feeling.' What she did say was, 'Another cup?' and he came and sat down too, and they ate toast and talked and it was pleasant and casual.

Halfway through Prudence's second slice of toast there was another tap on the door and Jake said, 'That's probably the papers.'

She gritted her teeth. Her father's death could be in the Sundays too, maybe the photograph again. Nobody would connect it with her, but she didn't want to read the headline or see the name in print. She wouldn't look at a newspaper today.

'Thanks,' said Jake, as John handed him folded papers at the door. 'Coffee?'

'No, thanks, I thought I'd get a breath of air.'

Prudence wondered if he was being tactful, by not intruding on his partner who was sharing a breakfast tray with a girl with whom he had obviously shared his bed, or if he really did feel like walking round the grounds. Perhaps he had things on his mind. Business matters, or a wife who looked twenty years younger than he did and whose whereabouts nobody seemed to know.

Jake came back, offering her the *Times* or the *Observer*, and she said, 'I'd better be walking home myself. It's past Percy's breakfast time.'

'He's all right. He can get in.'

'Through the cat flap, yes. But he likes having me around.'

'Of course he does, who wouldn't?' He smiled at her, and his voice was suddenly as intimate as a touch. 'I liked having you, very much,' and she thought, I don't want him to touch me because it's too late. If he kisses me I could lose all sense of time and John could reappear and when do the cleaners come?

She laughed, and sat back in her chair. 'Harking back to Percy, he's one of the reasons I don't want to sell the cottage. He's a creature of habit. It's his home, he wouldn't fancy an apartment, not even a super one like this.'

That got her off dangerous ground. The sale of her cottage mattered to Jake. He would discuss that any time. He might even find it more interesting than

making what would have had to be hurried love to
Prudence. Besides, Percy could be a reason. He was
only a cat, but he was hers, and the cottage was where
he had stopped running too.

'Then buy him another cottage,' said Jake, and for
the first time she found herself wondering why she
had imagined that only in Stable Cottage could she be
safe. 'You know,' she mused, 'I just might.'

'Good,' he said. 'You think about it.'

He turned to the front page and Prudence turned
the leaves of a colour supplement, thinking, not
reading. The moment she began to seriously consider
selling, all the arguments against seemed absurd. Once
there had been big important reasons for staying.
Nobody will make us run from here, she had vowed.
Here we are safe and here we will stay. But now she
only had herself to consider, and home could be
wherever she made it.

She had a feeling of liberation, as though she had
pushed a door that was always locked and it had
opened. Staying in Stable Cottage no longer seemed a
guarantee against heartache and the adventure of
finding somewhere new was growing more enticing by
the moment.

At the end of fifteen minutes Jake was still reading
the papers, they were still drinking coffee and eating
toast, and if he had asked her to sign a contract to sell
she would have signed. She had made up her mind,
and the next time the subject came up she would say,
'Right.'

This time there was no tap on the door from the
corridor. It simply swung wide and Tanya swanned
in. 'Do you have coffee in here?' she asked.

Jake lifted the empty pot. 'Sorry.'

John was behind her, wearing a dark blue track suit,
so he must have gone jogging. He was a little flushed,

and more than a little overweight, and Prudence
hoped he knew what he was doing. Tanya was glowing
too, but she wasn't dressed for jogging, in a pale
strawberry suit and soft leather boots. Radiant with
health and high spirits—maybe she *had* been at a
health farm, she could certainly have been an
advertisement for one.

She laughed, 'I nearly ran over my old man coming
up the drive. That would have been a fine thing,
wouldn't it?' John Merrick chuckled and sank down
into the nearest chair, patting his paunch with both
hands.

'I don't think this is working.'

'How long have you been jogging?' Prudence
enquired.

'Years,' he said lugubriously, so it wasn't working.
Jake looked lean and hard beside him, fitter and
tougher, and Tanya giggled as though Prudence had
voiced all this.

'No, Jake doesn't jog. Jake takes other forms of
exercise.'

'I know,' said Prudence, 'we went swimming.'

'Nothing beats an early morning swim,' said Tanya.
She perched on the arm of Jake's chair, and he looked
at Prudence and said, 'I wouldn't say that.'

'Wouldn't you now?' Tanya drawled. 'No wonder
you both needed black coffee!' She reached over to lift
the pot herself, opening the lid and peering in. If it
had contained hot coffee Prudence had the impression
that Tanya might have spilled it her way.

'Well, how did it go?' Tanya asked Jake, who
reasonably asked, 'What?'

'Your trip. You have just come back from France,
haven't you?'

'It went well,' he said.

'That's nice.' She dipped a spoon in the small jar of

apricot conserve and licked it like a child. Then her tongue flickered between her lips as though the taste of sweetness lingered, and her gaze flickered towards Jake, before she opened her eyes wide and began to talk about people of whom Prudence had never heard. She had spent last night at their home, she said, and perhaps she had, but she had left here four nights ago.

'I really must be on my way,' said Prudence when Tanya paused for breath. Jake got up too and Tanya said, 'I thought we might all have lunch together.'

'I'm sorry!' said Prudence quickly, 'but I can't.' She had sat through one meal with this foursome. It had not been a happy occasion and she had no wish for a repeat performance. She hoped her floundering was imperceptible before she went on, 'I've already promised to go over to friends for lunch.'

It would have been nice if Jake had said no, and maybe he would have done if Prudence had given him the chance. She had refused at lightning speed and it didn't seem to bother Tanya, who said brightly, 'Oh dear!'

Again Jake helped Prudence into her coat, but this time he didn't pull up the collar and kiss the tip of her nose, and she was very conscious of Tanya's little smile. 'You do look pale,' Tanya said solicitously. 'Have you been overdoing things?'

'No make-up,' said Prudence sweetly. 'You should try it some time.'

She didn't enjoy being baited, and Tanya really could rile her. She said 'Goodbye, then,' and as they walked down the curved staircase she told Jake, 'My purse is in the changing room, I won't be a minute.' She left him in the entrance hall, waiting for her, and hurried towards the pool.

It was glass-smooth again this morning, with the bubbling jacuzzi beside it, and she would have liked to swim again, but that wasn't the plan for today. Tanya was right, she did look colourless. Her reflection in the mirrored wall of the cloakroom was a pale wraith compared with last night, let alone compared with Tanya. Last night she had looked good, and the swimsuit had been flattering.

'Oh *hell*!' she groaned, grimacing, and she picked up her purse and retraced her steps. The front door was open, Jake was just outside, and she went across to him and mumbled, 'My swimsuit—er—do you know where it was left?'

He shook his head, and she muttered, 'I'll bet Tanya finds it.'

'Does it matter?'

'I suppose not.'

She was sure that Tanya would be prowling around and that the swimsuit would be by the bed. It was none of Tanya's business, but she wished she had remembered the blessed thing herself. Brilliant pink should have stood out, even if it was underfoot.

They were only a few yards from the house when one of the long windows, immediately over the door, opened and Tanya waved the swimsuit like a flag. 'Hey,' she called, 'catch!'

Prudence clenched her fists and scowled as the skimpy garment floated down. Jake picked it up, and Prudence called, 'How terribly kind of you.'

'That's me,' trilled Tanya. 'Nothing's too much trouble.'

'She's a nut case,' muttered Prudence, as Tanya closed the window, and Jake grinned,

'Her mind got stuck at ten years as well as her face.'

I don't think her mind got stuck, thought Prudence. I think she has the mind of a scheming woman, and much more of this and I'm going to ask her if she had a thrilling time with her husband, starting on Wednesday night.

It was ridiculous, letting Tanya get to her. Tanya was almost a joke. Tanya, as Jake had just said, did not matter. Prudence took a deep breath and put Tanya out of her mind. 'If I do sell,' she asked him, after a few moments, 'how soon would you want it?'

'The sooner the sale went through the better.'

'I think I might.' She had quite decided. She would be pleasing herself, but it was nice to be pleasing him too. 'I'll start looking around right away.'

'Do you want any help?' asked Jake.

'What sort?'

'Shall I come house-hunting with you?'

He would know all there was to know about property, but she could get expert advice enough for one small house and it would not be wise to go searching for her future home with Jake Ballinger. If he went with her, through all the rooms: kitchens, living rooms, bedrooms, he would be choosing it too, but he would be gone before she moved in.

They were reaching the end of the drive, turning towards the entrance to her cottage, and she said gaily, 'I'll know if I like it. You won't be living there.'

That struck her chill, although she smiled when he said, 'No.' You won't be haunting it either, she thought. 'Buy anything you need,' he said.

'Thank you. That's nice to know.' She was realising that she could begin to need too much from him, and she had been avoiding that kind of dependence for years. She held out a hand for the swimsuit he carried. 'Yours is one of the best pools I've ever encountered,' she told him.

'I'm so glad it was satisfactory.' They were almost at her door. His voice was serious, but his eyes were laughing.

'Yes—oh yes,' she said. 'Very satisfying. I had a perfectly splendid time.'

'We must do it again.'

This was double-talk. It was the lovemaking they were talking about; which had been expert and enjoyable for him, and so far as Prudence was concerned could have made her his slave for life. But he wasn't knowing that. 'Some time we must,' she said, smiling, smiling, thinking—Not tonight, not too soon. I'm not going blindly into that trap again. Because it was a trap, a sensual enslavement of body and mind, and surrender like that was a terrible risk to take.

'Would you mind explaining to Percy how I came to stay out all night?' she said. The cat was sitting on the grass beside the garage door, green eyes squinting. He looked mean and moody, which was his usual expression, but he usually came right away for Prudence. This morning he stayed put and glared. 'Good heavens,' she said, 'he *is* sulking! Look, buster, you stop out many a night. Do I put on a face like that in the morning? Do I even ask where you've been?'

She stroked him and a faint rumble came from deep in his chest. 'Is he growling?' Jake asked.

'Mostly purring,' said Prudence. 'He's a male chauvinist tomcat, but he usually listens to reason.' Jake chuckled, as she put her key in the door, and asked,

'These friends you've promised, can't you get out of it?'

'Not easily.'

She needed some space between herself and Jake for a little while, although if he had persevered she might have wavered. But he didn't. 'I'll see you tomorrow, then,' he said.

'Can we make it Tuesday?'

'Of course.' He didn't question her about Monday. He kissed her with a light sensuous brushing of the lips and said, 'You *are* too pale. You need the sunshine.'

'He tells me that,' she laughed, 'at the very beginning of winter!'

She went on laughing until the door was closed, and she stood in the hall and he was walking away from the house. Then she thought of him going back to John and Tanya and the only way she could stop herself opening the door and calling after him was by not moving a muscle. She clenched her fingers and stood stiff and straight, hardly breathing until he had to be out of the garden and walking up the drive to the Centre.

She felt she had done well. Look at me letting go, she thought, and she let herself relax and went into the kitchen. She had done no clinging. She had wanted to spend today with Jake, and tonight—of course she had wanted to stay with him tonight; but this was showing herself that she was her own woman. And that was the way to be, because Jake only considered her his woman on a very casual and temporary basis.

She warmed some milk to make Percy a bowl of instant porridge, one of his favourite breakfasts, and while he was lapping that up she went into the living room, to open the stove and stir the ashes and put another log on the fire. Then she picked up the newspaper. It lay where she had dropped it beside the chair, and she had intended to throw it away without looking at it again and try to forget it. Only she found herself looking at the photograph, her eyes brimming with tears, so it seemed that she could weep for him.

Perhaps not for the man who had died on Wednesday but for the father she had lost ten years ago, and the child she had been when this picture was

taken. The child was looking at the man with such
trust. Prudence would never again trust anyone so
completely, but she took scissors from her workbox
and cut out the photograph. She *would* keep it. There
had been happy days. She put it in an envelope and
dropped it into a drawer in the bureau, and said,
'Goodbye,' as she closed the drawer.

The story she couldn't read again. She crumpled the
rest of the newspaper and dumped it in the dustbin.
Anything else that was printed she would try to
ignore, and she would buy no papers today. The usual
delivery service didn't operate on Sundays, when the
post office-cum-newsagents was closed. Most of the
village went along and bought from a van on the
green, but maybe the van delivered to the Centre in
anticipation of a thumping big Sunday order in the
future.

She opened the local weekly at the property pages
and spread them out on her dining table, poring over
them. She wanted an old house. Not too rambling, she
would have to do the housework and she had to
consider the upkeep, and she pencilled round several
possibilities, including a couple from Bobby's firm.

She spent the day alone, driving round and getting
first impressions. She lunched by herself in a pub,
crossing out some of the places she had seen so far,
ticking others. No one who knew her came into the
bar, while she ate a steak and kidney pie with a baked
potato and drank a glass of white wine, but she got
some appraising glances that went right over her head.

She was used to being sized up and chatted up. She
was young, attractive, with undeniable style, and
chance acquaintances rarely made much impact on
her. A man sat down beside her and tried to start a
conversation, but she gave him no encouragement,
concentrating on her lunch and her property pages.

And when she finished eating she picked up her
handbag and newspaper and made her way out of the
bar in an unhurried direct line.

The light was fading when she reached the last
house, which was part of a coach house conversion.
Two units had 'Sold' notices up, the last remaining
still awaited a purchaser, and Prudence peered in
through windows, liking what she could see. This was
being handled by Bobby's firm and tomorrow she
would ask for a key.

Back home she went over them all again, in her
mind, sitting at her dining table, comparing and
considering. She was going to enjoy this, and from
now on she would take someone else along to house-
hunt with her. Sally maybe. Sally had a homemaker's
eye, but unfortunately not an eye for picking the right
man.

She would have to tell Jake, of course. There were
lights on in the Centre, and lights showing in her
cottage, and she had half expected him to ring her
because he could see she was home again, and had
been all evening. But nobody rang, and when she was
ready for bed she found herself dialling his number.

She had never rung it before. She didn't think she
knew it. But while she was having breakfast in his
room this morning the numbers on that phone must
have registered, because her finger clicked them off as
though she knew them well. She would see him
tomorrow night if he could make it. There was little
enough time left when he would be available and she
would be crazy to waste any of it.

His voice made her smile, although all he did was
announce the number she had just dialled. 'Hi,' she
said, 'it's Prudence.' She heard laughter than, faintly
in the background. 'Sorry, have you got company?'

'Only John and Tanya,' he said, and she felt he

should have said, 'Tanya and John,' because it had to be Tanya who was laughing, and somehow Prudence couldn't explain that she had changed her mind about tomorrow night and please could she meet him after all.

She said instead, 'I thought you might like to know I've been looking at houses. Only from the outside, but I'm sure I'm going to find something suitable very soon.'

He was interested, they talked for a few moments, but Prudence couldn't rid herself of the impression that Tanya was listening to every word, and hearing what Prudence was saying as well as Jake. When she hung up she looked at the little carriage clock on her mantelpiece and was surprised to see how late it was. Well after midnight. Time she was in bed; and high time that Tanya was out of Jake's room and into her own . . .

'I'm selling them the cottage,' Prudence told Sally as they opened the shop next morning, and Sally said, 'I should think you are! I could never understand you saying you weren't interested in such a fantastic price.' Her face fell. 'You won't be wanting the flat, will you?'

'I'm house-hunting,' Prudence reassured her, producing the newspaper pages. 'I took a first look at these yesterday. Will you come and help me choose?'

'Ooh yes,' said Sally. 'I love going round houses. One of these days I'll be looking for a house for myself.' She sighed. 'A family house,' she said firmly. 'That's what I shall want. You'll be wanting somewhere smaller, won't you?'

She meant that Prudence was a career girl, not the marriage-and-family type. But friends would come to stay, and some day Prudence might meet a man who

wanted to share her life and perhaps her home. And
she might feel the same about him. It was unlikely,
but it could happen. 'Not too much of a bachelor pad,'
she joked. 'Anyhow, I've got a family—Percy.'

'That cat!' Sally chortled. 'He's a wild one.'

'He's very domesticated,' said Prudence. 'He likes
everybody in at nights.' Her eyes were dancing, and
Sally giggled and thought she knew where Prudence
had been spending some of her nights.

Prudence phoned Bobby's office and asked for Mr
Bygrave, and the girl who took the call and recognised
her voice said, 'He's got somebody in with him now,
but I'm sure he'd like me to put you through.'

'It's business,' Prudence said hastily.

'Half a mo,' the girl chirrupped, then the phone
clicked and Bobby said, 'Bygrave here.'

'Prudence,' she said, 'about a house. I'm in the
market for one. I've decided to sell the cottage.'

'I thought you might.' His voice was cool. 'I
thought you'd be changing your mind.'

She could have told him, 'I think it was because of
my father. He was killed last week and that chapter
finally closed.' She said, 'I saw the coach house and I
liked the look of it, could I see round that?' and Bobby
became brisk and businesslike, assuring her that she
could, any time, and mentioning a property near
Jean's home that she might consider.

'I'll bring the details to the shop,' he said.

Prudence had hardly put down the phone when it
rang again. This time Tanya was on the other end. 'So
you *are* selling us your cottage—I *am* pleased! Didn't I
tell you Jake never takes no for an answer?'

'I believe you did,' said Prudence.

'I know how it's been bugging him,' said Tanya
gaily. 'He hates anything standing in his way, any little
detail he can't control. How did he persuade you to do

what he wanted?—No,' she shrieked, 'don't tell me how!'

'I wasn't going to tell you anything,' said Prudence, and banged down the phone. Then she swore at herself for losing her temper with Tanya yet again, and Sally asked, 'What on earth was that about?'

'Mrs Merrick,' said Prudence. There were no customers in the shop, but she would probably have spoken out just the same if there had been. The tone of Tanya's voice flicked her on the raw. Tanya was laughing at her; Tanya had been laughing at her right from the first. She said, 'Mrs Merrick thinks I haven't had a mind of my own since Jake homed in on me. Never takes no for an answer, does Jake, according to Tanya, and what he was after was my bit of land.'

'But that's not right,' cried Sally.

But of course, everybody else thought the same as Tanya. For months Prudence had been so determined she was not going to sell. She would listen to advice from no one, and then along comes Jason Ballinger and he and she become almost inseparable, and within a few weeks she changes her mind. Nobody else had been able to persuade her, but it was obvious that he had the knack. And a good thing too, her friends thought.

Even Bobby grudgingly admitted that the sale was in Prudence's interests as much as in Ballinger and Merrick's. Bobby arrived at the shop in the early afternoon, with several leaflets in his briefcase, and a professional air of courteous detachment. He wanted to sell Prudence a house, and he was prepared to see that she got a fair deal, and he hoped he was civilised enough to accept that when an affair was over it was over.

All the same, as he walked through the door, and she came to meet him, he couldn't help hoping that perhaps it wasn't quite over because he would always find her very attractive.

The coach house had converted into three pleasant homes, and Prudence was impressed. She could see her furniture in here, and she could afford the price with a little left over. She walked around, listening to Bobby's sales talk, and agreeing because anyone could see this was a desirable residence.

From there they went to the house under the hill of the stones, where she could walk up to Jean's in under five minutes. This was a Victorian house in a pretty garden, and she liked that too, and afterwards Bobby drove her up to the farmhouse to tell Jean that she was on the move, and could end up as a neighbour.

When they got out of the car Jean waddled from the back door to meet them, having spotted them through the kitchen window, and put her own interpretation on seeing Prudence and Bobby together again. 'This is a suprise, how lovely! Come on in.'

She was beaming. She had decided she was pleased because Jason Ballinger was a ship that passed in the night but Bobby Bygrave could turn into a fixture.

'How's Junior?' Prudence enquired, and Jean puffed out her cheeks in exasperation,

'If she doesn't get a move on I'm thinking of telling them to forget the whole thing.'

'We're house-hunting,' Prudence explained. 'We've been looking at the one in Scholars Lane,' and Jean swung round as fast as her bulk would allow.

'You two? Looking for a house together?'

'Bobby's selling, I'm buying,' said Prudence. 'I've decided to let the cottage go.'

'So somebody's been talking you round,' said Jean archly, and went on to say that it was good news, and what a good house the one in Scholars Lane was, and how she would love to have Prudence living there.

Prudence was teased. If she hadn't made such a stubborn stand her turnabout would have been less dramatic, but as soon as it got around that she was selling after all everybody thought that Jason Ballinger had swung it. And as nothing was going to convince them otherwise she didn't argue.

But it did rankle, although she was sure Jake had not had the cottage in mind all along. He liked her very much, or he wouldn't have spent so much time with her. They had got on marvellously well, with hardly a mention of her selling until she brought it up herself on Sunday morning.

In the first place, yes, he had come across to her when she was hang-gliding because she was the girl whose land he wantd to buy. He had shown her round the Centre, and offered her accommodation there, because she was the owner-occupier of Stable Cottage, but right away he had enjoyed her company. Right away they had hit it off. If there had been no cottage and they had just met in the village and remarked on the weather she thought they would have gone on talking, and the instant rapport between them would have developed along exactly the same lines.

On Tuesday the Ballinger and Merrick solicitors got in touch to ask who were Prudence's solicitors. She had never needed a lawyer, so she gave the name of a local firm, then rang through to ask them to act for her.

'They don't waste much time, do they?' commented Sally as Prudence replaced the receiver.

'Seems not,' said Prudence. She had a pile of properties, both from Bobby's firm and from three other estate agents, and she had a headache. The headache was unusual, she wasn't given to them, it was her mother who had suffered from headaches, but today a knot of tension had been building up at the back of her skull, tightening like a vice.

There was an article in the morning paper on people who disappear, how many did and how easy it was to do if you put your mind to it. David Sinclair's death had triggered that feature. There was a single-column photograph of him, not of Prudence this time, together with a head-and-shoulders of Lord Lucan and an M.P. called Victor Grayson, who was sipping a drink in a London hotel when he suddenly hurried out into the street, calling over his shoulder, 'Back in a minute', and never came back.

She hadn't read the article, but it had started the headache, and the mail had been full of bills and circulars and it seemed that everybody had heard about her selling her cottage to Jake. Nobody was surprised, but she was sick of the smiles. 'Did he make you an offer you couldn't refuse?' one customer joked, and Prudence said, 'Something like that.'

'I wish he'd make me one,' said the young woman, and Prudence went into the office and took another couple of aspirins. But when she got home the headache was still pounding. Her father's death must have affected her more than she had realised, and there was all the hassle of house-hunting and moving ahead. Some of the fun had gone out of that today, with everybody hinting that Jake had her eating out of his hand. It wasn't true, but it could be, and tonight she was drained. She didn't feel up to being bright and clever and watching her step.

She rang his number and he answered. If she hadn't been able to contact him he would just have arrived on her doorstep and she would have had to let him in. But she got him, so she said, 'About tonight, would you mind if I called it off? You might not believe this, but I've got a splitting headache.'

'Sorry to hear that,' he said. 'Why shouldn't I believe it?'

'No reason. I've taken pills and things and it's still thudding away, so I'm going to lie down.'

Jake said it was the best thing she could do. He sounded concerned, and Prudence told him, 'It doesn't often happen. Your solicitors phoned me today.'

'Yes.' He knew that.

'I've a sheaf of places. Tomorrow afternoon I'm going to look at some.'

'Go and lie down now,' he said.

Rest was the sensible thing. It was the only sure cure for a really rotten headache, and he didn't keep her talking. Not even long enough to fix another date. When she put down the phone she wondered if she would be seeing so much of Jake in the future, or if they could be right and the cottage could have been his main objective.

But he rang next morning before she left for work to ask how she was, and after a night's sleep the headache had gone. 'Dinner tomorrow night?' he asked.

'I'd like that. I'm house-hunting this afternoon.'

'Good luck.'

'I'll be lucky,' she said gaily.

She had woken early, and lain wondering when she was going to see him again, but of course he was still dating her. The sale of the cottage hadn't changed their friendship and she wouldn't listen to the things that were being said. After dinner tomorrow she would try very hard to stay cool, but she would make herself as glamorous as possible because it would be wonderful if she could shake Jake out of his self-control. It would be a little miracle if she could get under his skin so that he was no longer in total command of the situation or of himself.

That afternoon Prudence took Sally round the houses with her. The coach house was tempting and so was the cottage in Scholars Lane, and Sally was becoming dewy-eyed, sniffling slightly. 'It's lovely,' Sally sighed deeply as they stood in the kitchen of the conversion. 'It's horrible, isn't it, being alone? Well, you don't mind, do you? You manage all right, but I keep thinking how lovely it would be living here with Adrian.'

Sally was getting over Adrian. Another few weeks and she would have fixed her sights on another man, and then he would become the paradox of every male virtue, but this tour had made her melancholy and perhaps it hadn't been such a good idea after all. 'Well, I've narrowed it down to two,' said Prudence. 'Shall we take the keys back?'

She was still undecided, handing them in at Bobby's office just before six o'clock. Bobby opened his door, looking surprised to see her, although the door had been ajar and he had been listening for Prudence's voice. 'Come on in,' he invited the two girls.

'It's a toss-up,' she told him. 'I like both these.'

'We could talk it over. What are you doing this evening?'

She pleaded, 'I'm sorry, but I can't.' She was not taking up with Bobby again, she was just putting some business in his way, and he said before he could stop himself,

'I don't suppose it's Ballinger. You won't be seeing so much of him now he's persuaded you to sell the cottage.'

Her dark brows arched. 'Why shouldn't I be seeing him? As a matter of fact I'm having dinner with him tomorrow night.'

'Signed anything yet?' Bobby asked.

'I've told the solicitors I will.'

'Yes, well,' Bobby made that sound meaningful, and Prudence laughed at him. Outside on the pavement

Sally, said, 'Hasn't he got lovely eyes?' and Prudence
blinked. 'Bobby Bygrave,' explained Sally. 'They're
really soulful, aren't they?'

'They've always reminded me of a spaniel,' said
Prudence. 'Perhaps that's why Percy usually spits at
him.'

Tanya arrived at the shop on Thursday, in one of
her charming moods. She had, she told them, found a
rather gorgeous mirror for the boutique, and she
thought they should get down to discussing the stocks
they were opening with. Time rushed by at such a
rate, didn't it? Here they were, halfway through
November, and opening at the end of December.

Sally was still very taken with Tanya. After all, what
she had said about Jason Ballinger persuading
Prudence to sell had to be true; and she was being very
sweet and complimentary about Sally's knitwear and
Prudence's jewellery.

She picked up a charm, and it happened to be the
one Prudence was giving Jake. It was lying on the
desk, on tissue paper, and Sally said brightly,
'That's Jake's birthday present. Prudence made it
specially.'

Prudence could have flattened her. She wondered
why on earth she had *told* Sally. But it wasn't a secret,
and Sally had caught her smiling at it when she
finished it and asked, 'Is there anything special about
that one!'

'I made it for Jake,' Prudence had told her. 'It's his
birthday next week. I thought he might carry it in his
pocket for luck.'

Now Tanya said, 'So that's what you're giving the
man who has everything.' She grinned, 'Including the
cottage.'

'What are you giving him?' asked Sally, and Tanya
shrugged and went on smiling.

'Oh, I'll think of a present he'll like.'

'I'll bet you will,' Prudence muttered, and Tanya's eyes narrowed, and Prudence saw something in them that she couldn't place but that she found very disturbing.

CHAPTER SEVEN

'WELL,' said Prudence, looking at herself as she waited for Jake on Thursday, 'You're never going to look better.'

She was glowing with happiness, and it was hard to keep cool because when she thought about him she felt warm right to the tips of her fingers. She knew he was a hard man, but no one else generated his electric excitement.

When he knocked on the door she jumped out of her seat and ran. She stopped for a moment before opening the door, telling herself to calm down. She mustn't hurtle into his arms, that would look altogether too enthusiastic even if she did manage to turn it into a joke. But when she opened the door somehow she was in his arms. He must have stepped in, because they were in the hall and he was holding her very close, and she wanted to twine herself round him, like ivy on a tree, and grow with him.

'I never knew a girl who smelled so good,' he said.

'That's pricey stuff. It's supposed to smell better than "good".'

'Not that. Anyone can get that in a bottle.' His lips feathered her face. 'You,' he said. 'Everywhere.'

He should know. All her expensive perfume had been washed away when she lay in his arms. And what happened next could happen again, and it would if he didn't stop kissing her; her legs were going now.

'How about the Fourways?' he asked.

'To eat? Yes, that's always good, and not too far.' Of course they had to eat and the night was young, and he could hold her and kiss her without losing his head. She was the one going to pieces, and she was only glad that she could still sound sane and sensible. Later, when they came back here, it wouldn't matter if she flipped, but first they would talk over a dining table, and she would be bright and funny and nobody would know that she was burning up for him.

Tonight, except for what looked like a business dinner of four men, the dining room at the Fourways Hotel was empty. But the carvery was up to its usual standard and they sat with food and wine before them and smiled at each other.

They were early. Other tables filled, but Prudence hardly noticed. She could have been in the middle of a crowd with Jake, or on a deserted island, and both would have felt much the same. As though this man was all the company she needed and no one else mattered.

He made her laugh. He always did—this time telling her about an appalling meal he had once been faced with in Tibet, containing some unspeakable ingredients. Then he asked how the house-hunting was going and Prudence said, playing with her food, pushing it around with her fork, 'How important is my cottage to you?'

'It would be convenient to have the land.'

'Suppose I backed out?'

'Why?' She did *not* think it mattered that much to him, but she countered with another question.

'Could I?'

'Of course you could.' He was reassuring her that the choice was hers, and she grimaced at herself.

'I do want to sell, I really do. But they're saying you twisted my arm and I feel a bit of a fool.'

'Who says?'

'Bobby for one. You know Bobby, you've met him a

couple of times. He hang-glides and he's an estate agent.'

'And he comes when you whistle.'

'I didn't whistle, I phoned him—he's got houses on his books.'

'He would have.' Jake put on an evil leer. 'And he thinks I've been twisting your arm to get my wicked way?'

That made her laugh again, and after that she put all doubts about the cottage from her mind. Jake's 'wicked ways' with her had nothing to do with a petty little property deal; they were something far more satisfying and much more delightful. She would take him home with her tonight and he would stay. She knew that he would leave the village quite soon, but tonight would be hers and she would savour every shining moment of it.

When she got up from her chair the manager hoped they had enjoyed their meal, and that he would have the pleasure of serving them again soon, and presented Prudence with her flower. The delicate perfume of it made her want to retch. Her fingers closed stiffly on the stem as she said how pretty it was, a cream spray of double freesias, a flower she hated because there had been that bowl of freesias with the note propped up against it. The air in her parents' bedroom had been full of the scent of them, and they always brought back that scene when her mother laughed for the last time and turned into an old woman.

She would have thrown it away as soon as she got outside, but that would have meant explaining why. It froze her. It turned her heart to ice. The drive home only took minutes, and she said a few words and tried not to look at the flower she was holding. 'Please,' she said, as they came to her cottage, 'I've had a lovely evening and this is going to sound very ungrateful, but if I don't ask you in will you be mortally offended?'

'Not mortally,' said Jake.

He got out of the car with her, and she turned her key in the lock, chattering away, saying thank you several times, and then goodnight. He held her hand when he said, 'Goodnight.' But he loosed it and let her go, and once inside the house she could drop the freesias.

She wished she could have told him why she had suddenly changed, from being relaxed and happy and sexy into frozen frigidity. If he had insisted on coming in she might have started talking about it after a while.

She moved around, doing the late night chores automatically, wishing they had chosen any other flower for this week's give-away gimmick. It had been the shock of it that had shattered her. The scent of the perfume she was wearing had masked the freesias, she hadn't noticed what other women were getting, she hadn't been looking around, and then it was thrust at her.

It was a little while before she began to feel human again, and then she went to the phone. She didn't know quite how to start. Maybe, 'I'm sorry, I've had second thoughts, would you care for a coffee after all?' Or she could just walk up to the Conference Centre and try to explain why she had frozen on him. She could say, 'Is anybody using your pool right now?' That would be a peace-offering, he would get the message, and it wasn't all that late.

There was a light burning in the turret window, and another in a side window on the ground floor. If John and Tanya were in residence Prudence hoped they wouldn't come to the door. She was prepared to face it out if they did, but she could see no one through the window and she was relieved when she tried the side door and it opened. This was part of the kitchens and she was going straight up to Jake's room before her courage gave out, and if anyone else popped up on the way—well, it wouldn't be the first time that Prudence had breakfasted with Jake.

She went quietly, hurrying past the Merricks' suite, and opening Jake's door because she didn't want to make a noise, rapping on doors in the corridor.

Tanya lay on the big squashy sofa, wearing a cherry red towelling robe and nothing else. For a moment Tanya gasped, then her lips and eyes narrowed and she looked every day of her age and her voice was soft and venomous. 'Not tonight, sweetie.'

She must be the biggest fool breathing. She had been such a crass and credulous idiot. Prudence sat in darkness, hunched in a chair in her living room, gasping for breath as though the hounds of hell were after her.

She had given one great sob and then run, along the corridor, down the stairs, out through the kitchen door that she knew was open, and down the drive from the house. She had only stopped running to turn the key and get in here, and now she put her hands over her ears, although there wasn't a sound to be heard.

It wasn't the sounds she wanted to shut out. It was the sight of Tanya lying there that was burned into her brain. There were no two ways of interpreting that, she hadn't needed Tanya to tell her who was sleeping with Jake tonight. Jason and Tanya were lovers, and Prudence should have known, because the clues were all around.

Now everything took on a different light. Jason Ballinger had wanted the cottage, but Prudence Cormack had another use. She was a smokescreen. She was the girl in this port that Jason Ballinger was dating and making, so that John Merrick had no suspicions that Tanya was anyone's sleeping partner but his. Not Jason's, at any rate. He might wonder about other men, but never about Jason; and as Merrick was the one with the money and the power in this company it was in their interests to keep him fooled.

Everything, she thought, *everything* should have warned me. Tanya laughing at me, things Tanya said. Jason making such a show of going around with me in public, so that it was common knowledge right away that he was supposed to be attracted to me. Maybe he was. Maybe that was a bonus. I asked him to make love to me and there was no hesitating about that, and he probably meant me to stay the night so that John would find me there in the morning. Because Jason was the one Tanya had gone to meet last week. The companion who was so marvellous that anywhere would have been exciting with him.

Prudence had always known she was not the only woman in Jason's life. He had a past and he would have a future that did not include her, but she had never let herself think about them and, although it would have hurt to find any other woman in his room just now, finding Tanya was a sickening betrayal because it meant that Prudence had been set up from the start. Selected to help them cheat John Merrick, who might have his doubts about his wife's loyalty but had none about his friend and partner.

This room smelled of freesias. That one spray seemed to have filled the air, and Prudence thought, this is the second time I've been destroyed. But she had to stand up and move around, she couldn't stay huddled here all night. There was work tomorrow, people to face. Life had changed, but the trappings hadn't. She would carry on as usual, except that Jason

Ballinger had gone for good. She couldn't think of him
any longer as Jake. Jason was the jet-setting tycoon
who let nothing stand in his way. He had had a use for
her here as well as wanting her scrap of land, and he
could say goodbye to that, he was getting nothing
more from her.

She had to get some sleep. She could have used
some of the sleeping pills her mother had taken for
years, but there had been none in the house since her
mother died. She poured out a stiff whisky, carrying
bottle and glass to the window because she couldn't
bring herself to switch on the lights. The darkness was
kinder. She undressed and washed in darkness, her
eyes growing accustomed to it so that she was seeing
almost as well as the cat, that followed her around and
sat at the bottom of the stairs, watching her as she
went up to bed.

The whisky burned her mouth, making her cough
and splutter as she stood at the bedroom window, but
she gulped it down, although her throat was scalded so
badly that tears trickled down her cheeks.

There was no light in the tower room now and she
wondered what they were doing in there, what they
were saying. She wondered if Jason had seen her rush
pell-mell from the house. She hadn't seen him, but she
hadn't stepped into the room, just opened the door
and looked in, and Tanya had jerked up and the robe
had fallen from her and she had spoken in a sort of
hissing whisper.

If Jason hadn't seen Prudence Tanya would have to
tell him, because Prudence wasn't going to be a
smokescreen any longer. She could go running to
John. John wasn't there tonight, that was sure enough,
but she might tell him as soon as she could. A woman
scorned would be expected to cause trouble.

And so I might, thought Prudence, damn them,

damn them. She could see into that dark room over there as clearly as though she stood beside them. She could see Tanya as she had just seen her, and she could see Jason as she had seen him a few nights ago. This night the lovemaking would not be all they had on their minds. They would have talking to do. Their cover was blown, they would have to decide how to deal with that, and Prudence should think herself lucky that she had found out. It was a nasty shock and a wretched business, but now she knew that Jason Ballinger's attraction for her had been at least ninety per cent sexual. She was not deeply involved. Maybe she had no heart to give, and wouldn't that be the best way to be, when you couldn't trust anyone and least of all the men who said they loved you? Not that he ever had said that.

The whisky fumes were reaching her brain, dulling the pain, taking her out of self-pity into a steely determination that she had done dancing to Jason Ballinger's tune, and it was now time for him and Tanya to pay the piper.

She woke late and feeling horrible. She wasn't sure whether her nausea was a hangover, or the memory of last night, but the house still smelled of freesias, and she went out, clutching her dressing gown around her, and dropped the flowers into the cold wet grass. Then she came back and very slowly and deliberately began to get herself ready for work.

She had been taken for a bigger fool than Bobby and the rest thought. They imagined that Jason had gone to all that trouble just to get her to sell her cottage, but what a juicy scandal she could start if she told them, 'Jason Ballinger is having an affair with his boss's wife. All these girls—like me—that he's seen around with are to stop John suspecting that his secret love is Tanya.'

She could face that this morning with no more than a feeling of contempt and disgust. Lord, she despised them! She hoped she never had to see either of them again, and when there was a knock on her door as she tried to get down a cup of black coffee, she stood back against the kitchen wall, refusing to answer. Then Tanya looked through the kitchen window and gestured, 'Let me in.'

'On your way,' Prudence mouthed back, and Tanya shook her head. If she stayed there, there would be a confrontation as soon as Prudence stepped outside, and she thought she would prefer it indoors. So she opened the door and said, 'Please be brief, I'm late.'

Tanya was wearing a bright pink track suit and Prudence wondered if she jogged with John and if he did, sometimes, wonder about her relationship with Jason. 'Well?' she said.

'It looked bad last night, didn't it?' Tanya had the rueful expression of a small girl caught in a small misdemeanour.

'From where I stood, yes,' said Prudence tartly. 'From where you were it probably looked very good. Have you come along to explain all on your own?'

She would have hated Jason to turn up too, but she was surprised that he was letting Tanya deal with this. 'He didn't see you,' said Tanya. 'He doesn't know you came.'

'Didn't you tell him?' That was astounding. She had expected Tanya to be thrown into panic, not to spend a blissful night in her lover's arms without warning him that tomorrow all hell could be let loose.

'You got the wrong idea,' said Tanya. 'I'd just been swimming.'

Tanya's hair had been fluffy as spun silk, she had come from no swimming pool; and even if she had, lying around naked in an unfastened robe on Jason's sofa meant only one thing. She must imagine that Prudence was so besotted with Jason that she was desperate for any explanation, or that Prudence was thick as a plank.

'So had I,' said Prudence, and anger twisted inside her so that a red mist rose before her eyes. 'And afterwards we both seem to have ended in the same place.'

Tanya's eyes narrowed and her mouth tightened, as it had last night when she saw Prudence walk into that room. It was jealousy and oh, how it aged her! She was the one who really had Jason, but she still resented the other girls, even if they did make the cheating safe for her. She snapped, 'You knew you weren't the only one.'

'Of course,' Prudence drawled. 'But I didn't realise I was playing the part to fool your husband,' and that shut Tanya up for about five seconds, which seemed a long time as the two girls stood facing each other in the kitchen. Then Tanya said, in what sounded like grudging admiration, 'You're smart.'

'I am from now on,' Prudence retorted, and Tanya chewed on her lip and tried another tactic, actually pleading,

'I knew Jake before I married John, we've always been very—er—good friends.'

She had married the wealthier man and lusted for the one who was infinitely more charismatic; and up to now she had got the best of both worlds. 'That's all it is,' she said, 'honestly. We fancy each other and we like each other, but we wouldn't do anything to hurt John, either of us.'

'Besides,' said Prudence, 'he has the money.'

'Yes, he has.' Tanya seemed to be admitting that reluctantly. 'He could break Jake. Do you want that?'

'I wouldn't lose any sleep over it,' Prudence said wearily.

'You wouldn't tell John, would you?' Tanya tried a little laugh, but this time it sounded nervous. 'Not that he'd believe you, of course.'

'You'll have to wait and see,' said Prudence. 'Both of you. In the meantime both of you keep away from me. And——' She had been going to add, 'The deal over the cottage is off' but she would save that to tell Jason. That would be a small slap in the face for him while she decided whether to deliver the knock-out blow and tell John Merrick.

It would have been easy to have phoned Sally and taken the day off, because Prudence really did feel ill. She could have taken to her bed and shut out the world, because the world was rotten and she was weary of it. But after Tanya had left, jogging down the garden path and presumably back to the Centre and Jason—now she would *have* to tell him—Prudence got into her car.

She passed the motorist, who watched out for her each morning, sooner than usual. She was later and driving fast to make up time, and she remembered that first meeting with Jason and how he had moved into her mind and obsessed her thoughts. He was dynamic, no doubt about that. Strong and ruthless and callous, and she doubted if he loved Tanya or anyone, but she was convinced that their affair had been going on for years. Maybe the risk gave it an added spice. Maybe they got a kick out of fooling poor old John Merrick.

The only way Prudence could handle this was by getting away from it. Not running in the physical sense, but retreating in every other way. She had had practice in both, and now her defences were higher than ever. She could have been wounded to the heart, if she had had a heart.

Sally greeted her cheerfully and right away began

talking about the houses they had seen yesterday. 'I loved them both,' she said. 'If you got either of them in the place of your cottage you'd be doing very well.'

Prudence was starting to say that she had changed her mind again, but she bit her lip, stopping the words, because this would be spiting herself as much as Jason. She did want a better house and a good price for the old one, and she was not going to be a loser all the way.

Instead she said, 'I will be doing well, won't I?'

'How did you get on last night?' Sally asked, smiling, and Prudence looked blank.

'What? Oh yes, we went out to dinner. It was very nice. We went to the Fourways.'

'I went there with Andrew,' Sally recalled. Andrew was the one before Adrian. Sally had thought he was sensitive and artistic and misunderstood. In fact he was a mother's boy and bone idle, and everybody knew that but Sally, until his mother put paid to the relationship. And who am I to talk? thought Prudence; my judgment's no better. I came near to trusting Jason Ballinger as blindly as Sally trusts her Andrews and her Adrians.

'They give you flowers, don't they?' Sally reminisced on. 'I had a pink rosebud. What did they give you?'

'A spray of freesias.' She could smell them now.

'Lovely scent, haven't they? When are you seeing him again?'

Prudence's shrug was elaborate. 'I don't know.'

'He didn't ask for another date?' Sally did hope it wasn't true about the cottage being all Jason Ballinger really wanted, but Prudence did look waxen pale, and Sally blurred, 'Is everything all right? You do look rotten.'

'I overslept,' said Prudence. 'And I didn't do a very

good make-up job. I think I'd better put on some more colour.'

In the little cloakroom she applied lipstick and blusher. She would let the sale of the cottage go through, and open the boutique. From now on everything was a business deal and she would never lose her head again. Only her pride had been hurt, and she could set about salvaging that.

She worked in her workroom all morning, trying out new designs on her sketchboard, until it was Sally's lunch hour. She heard the phone ring as she walked into the shop and then Sally came out of the office. 'It's for you.' Sally sounded as though she was handing over a very acceptable gift. 'It's Jake, shall I hang on?'

She meant while Prudence took her call, in case Prudence wanted to talk for a while. But this call was going to be brief, so Prudence said, 'That's all right,' and went slowly into the office while Sally ran up the stairs to her flat.

Prudence shut the office door behind her, then she picked up the phone, and said, 'Good morning.'

'When am I seeing you?' asked Jason.

'You're joking.'

'Am I?'

'Hasn't Tanya told you?'

'What are you talking about?' Tanya couldn't have done. Or perhaps he left early before Tanya saw Prudence. Perhaps Tanya had actually imagined she could talk Prudence into believing that she could be lying around naked in Jason's room and theirs could still be a platonic relationship. Fooling John all these years must have given her delusions about fooling everybody.

'Ask her,' said Prudence.

'I'm asking you.'

There was no anger in her. There was hardly any bitterness. She felt cold and contemptuous, and she said, 'You should lock doors,' and put down the phone.

It rang again at once, which she should have expected. This time she put it on the desk and came out of the office. Jake would realise what she had done and then he would probably ring Tanya. After that, even if he did try to get in touch with Prudence again, he must surely realise it was a lost cause.

She was not suffering. She was in control of her emotions now. She chatted with several customers she served during the next hours. Those who knew her personally were still on the subject of the cottage she was selling to Ballinger and Merrick after all. They wanted to know where she was going when she moved out, and that was probably the main thing on Bobby's mind too, because he turned up a few minutes after Sally came back from lunch and asked if Prudence had eaten.

'I'm just going along to the Kitchen for a bowl of soup,' she told him.

Gertie's Kitchen was a health food shop a few doors away, with a cheap and cheerful snack bar, and although Prudence was not hungry she mustn't start starving herself, because she could never afford to be ill.

'I'll come,' said Bobby eagerly. 'They do a good line in soups.'

The soup was delicious, but Prudence hardly tasted it. She sat beside Bobby at one of the little tables, with their red check gingham cloths and thick brown pottery, and tried not to think about last night and her last meal with Jason. No wonder he had been understanding about being sent on his way instead of invited in. Tanya was waiting, and what man in his senses wouldn't prefer Tanya? If Prudence had been just a little more deeply involved how she would have hated them both.

Bobby was talking and Prudence tried to look interested, and Bobby asked, 'Thought any more about your house?'

'The cottage in Scholar's Lane, I think.'

That kept them occupied, discussing formalities of the transaction, until the meal was nearly over, when suddenly Bobby said, 'About Ballinger——'

Prudence knew what he was going to ask and if she had tried to speak right away she might have choked. She had to swallow, and then take a few more sips of her cooling coffee, while Bobby stumbled over his question, 'Are you—I mean, will you still be seeing as much of each other? He's a fool if you don't but—well, do you think you will?'

'No,' said Prudence. She wasn't up to pretending, and it was better that they accepted this reason for the break-up. She actually smiled. 'It's hard to keep up with his sort. He's covered too much ground in his time.'

'Sure he has,' agreed Bobby. He hesitated again, wondering whether to press his luck, and ask her for a date, but perhaps it would be wiser to wait, he wouldn't rush it.

Her cottage was a cash sale, which meant they could get moving on her next home right away, and Bobby went back to the office to start the purchasing process. He was in good spirits and Prudence was pleased that one of his houses had been best of her list, but she hoped he was pinning no hopes on her split with Jason Ballinger because she had just had every prejudice in her nature reinforced. She had found it hard enough before to let any man get close to her. From now on it would be impossible. She was as ringed with thorns as the hedge round her cottage.

It was dark when she got home. She had stayed late at work, trying for a new design, because as well as a new house she would have liked something fresh and different in her work too. She was jaded, she supposed. All the bubbling enthusiasm had gone and left her feeling nothing at all.

She turned on the hall light and Percy came out of the living room. Prudence said, 'Hello,' and stroked him lightly then tensed, crouched over the cat. She knew he was here, in the darkened room, and for a moment her eyes flickered in panic towards the outer door. She wanted to run again, but she straightened and took the few steps that brought her to the living room, where Jason Ballinger stood, waiting.

He had remembered about the key under the stone, and that was the last time she would leave it there. She took off her coat and dropped it on a chair, on top of her handbag, then she said, 'Go away, will you?'

'You were at the Centre last night.' So Tanya had eventually told him.

'Briefly.'

'And you saw Tanya in my room.'

Back came the scene, sharp in every detail. She seemed to have a photographic memory for scenes that she would give her eye teeth to forget. 'Yes,' she said. 'Stark naked, except for the robe that wasn't fastened, so talk yourself out of that.'

'Tanya wants what she can't have,' he said. 'Always has.'

'And that's it?' She gave a derisive hoot. 'Hers was better. She said she'd been swimming.'

'I think she had.'

'She must keep her head high.' He must think she was so stupid. 'Look,' she said, and the contempt came through although she was trying to control herself in every way, 'I really don't care. Each to his own lifestyle.'

Jake would be a good poker player, you could never guess what he was thinking; and at last he said, as though this was nothing personal, as if they were discussing a business matter. 'It would be asking rather a lot to ask you to trust me.'

Trust him? Take his word that Tanya had lolled around naked and gone away untouched? If she believed that she would believe anything. 'Oh, it would,' she said. 'It would be asking much too much. It's been nice knowing you, but from now on it's strictly business.' She poked the fire that didn't need poking. Jake had opened the stove and stirred the ashes, and she wondered how long he had been here. 'I've found a house,' she told him. 'You can have the cottage any time. I suppose I still get to open the boutique?'

'Of course.'

'So that's it.'

'So it seems.'

As he took a step away she said, 'You're not afraid I'll tell John Merrick? That seemed to be Tanya's main concern.'

'He wouldn't believe you.' He spoke with confidence and she wondered if he was bluffing.

'So somebody trusts you,' she said savagely, and he looked straight into her eyes and, although she was in the right and he was in the wrong, her gaze dropped first and she was the one who turned her head.

The following Wednesday a letter arrived at Stable Cottage from the legal firm that was acting for her, saying they would be glad to see her any time to deal with the papers for transferring her freehold to the firmf of Ballinger and Merrick, who had already forwarded the deposit and dealt with their part of the contract.

'I hope you'll get used to it,' she said to Percy as she put down his breakfast saucer. 'We'll get a cat flap in before we move.'

It would be good to be living so near to Jean and her family. She had always like the village with the stones, and as she passed the two that leaned over the roadside she said, 'Hello, neighbours.' She passed the apprehensive motorist too, he was still working at the Centre. In a few weeks he and the rest of his team would be leaving the district, and Prudence wondered if she should reassure him that she was not a menace on the roads. That had been a one-off incident, and her time of madness was over.

She phoned and made her appointment from the shop. Then she phoned Jean and they chatted like old times. Jean didn't ask about Jason, although it had to be local knowledge that he hadn't been seen around with Prudence Cormack since she had agreed to sell him the cottage.

Prudence had neither seen nor heard from him. She heard the helicopter one morning, as she came out of the house to get into her car, but she didn't look up. On Monday it had been his birthday, and she knew now what Tanya had meant about a gift that he would like. There was no question of Prudence sending the little star-sign charm. He had had enough from her, and she had a bad day and a worse night because, although she would get over him and the way he had treated her, completely, eventually, she was still depressed about it.

She wasn't showing anybody that, though. She might not have been a born actress, but she had been acting most of her adult life, and now she carried on with her life, more or less as she had before she fell out of the skies at Jason Ballinger's feet.

She didn't stay in in the evenings, but she didn't date anyone in particular. She worked hard. The boutique was finished up at the Conference Centre. Tanya had come into the shop, looking apprehensive but relaxing when Prudence greeted her civilly. Prudence disliked most things about Tanya Merrick, but Tanya's morals were no concern of hers. All Prudence wanted from her was a reasonable attitude over the boutique, and there she seemed happy to give them a free hand.

It was looking very attractive. Tanya had produced a huge baroque mirror that made the little shop seem larger. It was carpeted now, with shelves and stands and counters, and Tanya agreed with all the stock they suggested, pronouncing everything lovely.

When the Centre opened, in the first week in January, Sally and Prudence would take turns to staff it during the evenings. The conference clientele would be occupied during 'working hours.' Jason would have gone by then, surely, and even if he had not Prudence was sure that it wouldn't bother her. It was almost five weeks since she had seen him, and their time together had been less than a month. Such a brief affair, ending so finally, really counted for nothing at all.

She never expected to see him again, and then the invitation arrived to the Christmas party. It was sent to the shop and signed by John Merrick, addressed to Prudence and Sally—a get-together for some of those who had worked on the conversion, the staff that would be taking over, and a few management personnel. Prudence might have found an excuse, but Sally said gently, 'I don't suppose you really want to go, do you? Jake will be there, I suppose, and everybody will understand if you don't feel up to facing him.'

'Of course I shall go,' said Prudence. 'Why should I

mind facing him?' She smiled because she didn't mind.

'Of course,' said Sally, 'he might not come.'

They took stock along that week, filling the shelves and dressing displays, and for the last few days a huge sparkling Christmas tree had stood in the entrance hall, reaching as high as the gallery. The house was busy with comings and goings, but Prudence saw neither the Merricks nor Jason Ballinger. Not that she wandered around. She confined herself to the boutique. The new manager introduced himself as Terry Mumford, with a flash of white teeth, and was called away immediately on another matter. Everything was ready for the old house to embark on is new career as a high-powered upmarket conference centre.

The night before Christmas Eve there was more than a sprinkling of snow. Sally and Prudence changed at Stable Cottage. Sally was wearing a winter-scene sweater, snowflakes and red-nosed snowman on a French navy background, and a navy knitted skirt. Prudence's outfit was a silken knit silver-grey suit, grey suede court shoes and her moon pendant. 'Very elegant; Sally had declared. 'But then you always look elegant. You don't think a touch of colour somewhere would be a good idea?'

Prudence did not. She didn't want to stand out in any way, because at least half the guests there tonight would know about her and Jason Ballinger. Most of the future staff were locals, and the invitation had included a partner, so that went double. They would be watching Prudence's reactions, and so would Tanya Merrick, no doubt. She didn't want to be conspicuous enough to catch Jason Ballinger's eye either. She wouldn't think about him, but she was sure he would carry off their meeting with complete aplomb, say, 'Hello,' and, 'How are you?' and then circulate, playing

the host with skill and charm. She just didn't want to
feel his eyes on her. She didn't want to look round
and find him looking at her.

This outfit was protective clothing. She was trying
to turn into a shadow that would merge into the
background, but she could hardly explain that to
Sally. Nor to Bobby, when he turned up to drive them
the three-minute trip to the Centre. He was not
Prudence's partner. She wasn't taking anyone, and
when Sally queried, 'Not even Bobby Bygrave?' and
Prudence had said, 'No,' Sally had asked, 'Would you
mind if I asked him? He's been saying he'd like to see
inside the Centre. Do you think it would be an awful
cheek?'

'Be my guest,' said Prudence, and although Bobby
took it as a joint invitation he had Sally to thank.

All the lights were on. The Centre was ablaze with
them, and there were plenty of cars in the forecourt.
Music was playing though loudspeakers and the
entrance hall was full. She had never seen a fire
burning in the big fireplace till now. Above hung a
modern painting of abstract shapes, and she remembered the first time she stood in here when she
had asked Jason Ballinger if his portrait would hang
there, dominating this hall.

He stood, with John and Tanya Merrick, by the
fireplace, and he dominated. He was probably the
tallest man there, but it was more than that. He was
looking across when she looked down from the
painting and a shock ran through her like touching a
live wire. It left her tingling, feeling rushing back into
what had been emptiness, and she knew she had been
fooling herself because time was not helping at all.
There would never be a time when she would not
want this man, fiercely and completely and to the
exclusion of all others.

She should not have come. Her only chance was to keep out of his sight because, even now, he was drawing her closer. The manager, debonair in evening dress, was greeting the newcomers at the door and Sally was introducing him to Bobby; and Prudence thought she was moving towards the fireplace. But it seemed that it was Jake who was coming over, because when he said, 'Hello,' she was still with Sally and Bobby, just inside the door. 'How are you?' he asked.

'Very well,' she said. 'Very well indeed. And I can see there's no need to enquire about your health.'

Now she began to circulate. Somebody handed her a drink and she was tempted to knock it back, but she had to keep a clear head. All the rooms on the ground floor were open, gleaming furniture and lush carpeting. She hadn't seen them quite ready before. On her last visit to the boutique they were beginning to bring in the furniture, and now she went around like a sightseer, like most of the rest were doing.

And Jason Ballinger went with her. Prudence hardly spoke to him, just enough to give the impression of being at ease, because she was being watched. She did ask, 'Whose benefit is this for?' quietly, smiling at someone she knew a little distance away.

'Mine,' he said, and she still didn't look at him.

'That figures,' she said.

The boutique had a glass door and a jewellery stand just inside with her star-signs as the centre piece. His charm was there, the Scorpio, and she had a wild impulse to say, 'See that? I made it for you. Did you enjoy Tanya's gift? Is she so much better than I am?'

Tanya hadn't spoken to her. She was talking and laughing with almost everybody else, she looked quite radiant, but her path and Prudence's hadn't crossed. John Merrick had said how nice it was to see Prudence again and that he was sure the boutique would be a success, and Prudence kept moving.

She wondered if he knew that she hadn't seen Jake again until tonight. She wondered if Jake was keeping close to her now to bolster an impression of togetherness, and how he had the effrontery to risk her making a scene. Maybe he thought the boutique would stop her, she had a little stake in the Centre. Or that she was too reserved—forgetting the swimming pool episode—to make a public spectacle of herself.

Eventually she would tell him to push off, drop dead, go *away*. As soon as they had a moment out of earshot of the rest. In the meantime she kept walking. The dining room had a buffet of quite spectacular proportions and a bar was providing unlimited drinks. Prudence took another glass, but she couldn't have eaten anything. There was ice clinking in the glass. She lifted it and looked at it, and Jake queried, 'A toast?'

'Success,' she said, because others at the bar were waiting to hear what she was going to say. 'And you don't need to drink to it.' He didn't have a glass anyway. 'You *are* it.'

He looked as he had always looked, with the red glints in his hair and the bronze tanned skin, and the power and the strength that would always carry him to success. And I, she thought drinking deep, am the moon witch who flew too near the sun, and ended up burned and scorched and seared to the soul.

'Lovely party,' she said, 'Lovely house. You'll be leaving here now, won't you?'

'No.'

She was out of the dining room, heading down the corridor that led to the library. She had been everywhere now except the sports area and the swimming pool. That was where a good number of the guests would end the evening, but not Prudence.

When Jason said no she gulped, 'Not leaving?'

'I'm keeping the apartment on,' he explained. 'It's convenient. I like it.'

That meant she could be seeing him any time, tonight was not the end of it, and her head began to swim because she couldn't stand it. She wanted to hate him, she did hate him, but she knew that if he really tried she would go into his arms any time he opened them to her. Hating herself but helpless.

The library was empty. There wasn't much to see in here: glass-fronted bookcases filled with reference books, chairs, tables, a couple of side lights burning. As she stepped inside Jake asked, 'How's your house-moving going?'

'Next month,' She had to tell him to keep away. He knew why, but she mustn't sound desperate, just determined.

'You've explained to Percy?'

Was that a joke? Were they joking? She said, 'Oh yes—yes, of course. I've promised him a cat flap before we move. He tipped the balance in the end. The next-best house was in a row, and Percy doesn't like people.' She added inanely, 'And not many people like Percy, and nobody loves him but me.'

'He must limit your lovers.' Jake was smiling, they *were* joking—and then he stopped smiling and put a hand on her shoulder and she clapped a hand across her mouth, screaming at him through it.

'Don't touch me! Don't come near me! Don't think I won't tell John Merrick that you and Tanya are cheating him and how you used me, don't think I won't!'

She couldn't get through the door because he was standing in her way. There were long windows leading into the garden and she ran to them and fumbled with the catch, and saw the falling snow outside and, reflected in the dark glass, the man sitting in the highbacked chair. And she knew before she turned that it was John Merrick.

CHAPTER EIGHT

SHE hadn't meant this to happen. She would never have told John Merrick that his partner and his wife were two-timing him, and she almost sobbed, 'I'm sorry,' fumbling with the latch of the patio doors again, 'but you must have known.'

John Merrick was no fool and it had been plain from the beginning. Prudence should have seen it herself from that first day she was introduced to Tanya. She couldn't look at either man, she had to get outside. The doors opened and she ran out, just as she had escaped from Jake's room that night, in headlong flight.

Snowflakes were whirling down. There was a thick carpet of them underfoot, soft and clogging, and the landscape was eerily white under a bright moon. She knew he was following her, although she couldn't hear him, and she ran as if she was running for her life.

When she trod on uneven ground under the smooth snow, and sprawled face down, she was up again at once, snow in her eyes and mouth but still running. Only then he was on her, grabbing her, shaking her, shouting at her, 'Listen to me, damn you!'

He was making her head jerk like a rag doll's. 'I'm sorry,' the words were being jolted out of her, 'sorry for John, I didn't mean him to hear me, but you two sicken me!'

'I am not having an affair with Tanya.' Jake seemed to be shaking her still at every word. 'Tanya is a mischief-maker, a stirrer. As far as I'm concerned she's a godalmighty bore and always has been, but

John's fond of her. And she's fond of him, although that doesn't stop her carrying on like an alleycat.'

He towered over her. She was numb with cold, but the pain of his grip was nearly paralysing her and she spat, 'So what do you want me to do? Go back there and tell him I made a mistake and I can't believe my own eyes? She said he could break you. Is that what's bothering you?'

'You're an absymal idiot!' He almost flung her from him and his voice was acid-edged. 'Do as you like, I couldn't care less.'

This time she knew he was not following. She ran across the snow-covered lawns towards the drive, keeping to the side, skirting the trees. The snow was still falling, her shoes were sodden and she was soaked to the skin. A shoe slipped off and she groped for it in the drift, and after that she went as fast as she could, but no longer rushing blindly. Just stumbling through the snow, making for home.

Snowflakes melted on her face so that it was wet, and she was gasping for breath, almost choking. When she reached her own front door and fell against it it was almost as though she was sobbing her eyes out.

She had dropped her purse somewhere, probably in the library, and she had to dig with frozen fingers in the snow to find the stone that hid the spare key. She had left the key there. Perhaps she had hoped, deep down, that Jake might use it again and be waiting for her one night and give her another reason why Tanya was in his room. Well, he just had. Tanya Merrick had the morals of an alleycat, but as far as he was concerned she was an almighty bore.

Prudence opened the stove and began to get out of her clothes in the warm glow from it. They fell to the floor like a pile of wet rags, and she turned on the water and wrapped the biggest bath towel she had around herself, waiting for the bath to fill.

It was believable. It could be like that. But if it was Jake would not forgive her for that scene in the library, because now John Merrick would be bound to believe the worst. She had destroyed what might have been a very good relationship between herself and Jake. Not all that long-lasting, of course, although he wasn't going away just yet, but she had poisoned it and he had looked at her out there in the snow as though she was poison.

The hot water warmed her, but when she got into bed she began to shiver again. She remembered the last time he was here, in this house, and how he had said. 'It would be asking rather a lot to ask you to trust me.' 'Much too much,' she had said. Now she said, 'Try me, help me,' and it turned into an agonising dream of what might have happened.

'Are you awake?' Sally whispered several hours later. Prudence had left the door unlocked, she had heard Sally come in and tiptoe upstairs. Now Sally stood by her bed, and she raised herself on an elbow, yawning, pretending.

'We went swimming,' said Sally. 'It was super! There were swimsuits, it was lovely.' She giggled. 'Although Tanya might as well not have been wearing one—she had these little bits of ribbon. Honestly, she has got a nerve! Who ran you home?'

'I ran myself,' said Prudence, and put her face back in the pillow. But she was still awake when Sally got into bed, and at last she heard Sally's soft rhythmic snores.

Sally was carrying a tray of crumbs out for the birds next morning when John Merrick jogged round to the kitchen door, and Prudence sat down suddenly on the high stool. She had been rushing around till now, but this was going to be grim, and she was wishing that Sally had gone home to her own flat last night.

'It was a lovely party,' said Sally.

'Glad you enjoyed it.' He was smiling, looking cheerful, puffing slightly from the exercise. The snow was crisp this morning and Sally walked around outside, scattering her crumbs far and wide. Percy was behind a closed door in the living room, and Prudence thought, I must leave him in there or he'll be catching a bird. She said, 'Good morning,' to John Merrick and was wondering what to say next when he produced her purse from his pocket and put it on the table. So she said, 'Thank you,' and then, watching Sally through the window, 'I'm sorry about last night.'

Merrick glanced towards the window too, but Sally couldn't hear them. She was concentrating on making a pattern of footsteps in the snow. '*I'm* sorry,' he said, 'By the way, Jake doesn't know I'm here, and I'd rather you didn't mention it if you see him again, but—you were wrong.'

She was glad to hear him say that. It meant she had done no lasting damage by her hysterical outburst, except incur what could be Jake's lasting contempt.

'Tanya, you see,' John Merrick went on, 'looks on her sexual attraction as her collateral, her money in the bank. As long as she can keep proving to herself she's irresistible she feels secure. Jake's always been her biggest challenge. She'd do almost anything to add him to her collection, but I know that she never will.'

'Her *collection*?' Instinctively Prudence grimaced. 'Don't you mind?'

'Not too much.' He shook his head, at himself it seemed. 'I'm not Jake, I don't have his standards, I don't have his strength.' He grinned ruefully, 'Come to that, I don't have his brains nor his drive. Nor his money.'

His money? 'Aren't you the senior partner?' she asked, and John Merrick chuckled at the very thought,

'Good lord, no! Jake's the boss man, I'm just an architect.' And that was another of Tanya's lies spiked.

'Merry Christmas,' said John Merrick, doing a few jogging steps in the doorway as Sally skirted him to get back in.

'Will you spend Christmas at the Centre?' Sally asked.

'No, we're leaving now.'

'All of you?' Sally persisted. 'Jake too?'

Jake, John told them, was spending Christmas and the New Year with friends in Scotland. So am I, with friends, thought Prudence. She was going to the Howards, as she had done every Christmas for years. She wondered what Jake's friends were like and wished they could be together, with a longing that ached as though she was sickening for an illness.

That day, Christmas Eve, was a good day for trade. Customers came buying last-minute presents. Outside carols pealed unceasingly from loudspeakers in the square. The streets were crowded and from time to time small flurries of snow drifted down.

And Jean had her baby. They had been serving mince pies and glasses of mulled wine to the customers, so that most of them hung around longer than necessary over their purchases; and as most of the customers were friends there was a pleasantly festive atmosphere in the shop. Prudence took the phone call, and it was Jean's mother to tell her she had a godson, born at home, no complications, and mother and child were sleeping peacefully.

Prudence squealed. 'Sally, the baby's come! Jean's baby's here!' So then everyone had another helping of mulled wine, and Prudence had to rethink the silver bracelet she had been taking along tomorrow for Jean's daughter. Jean had been convinced the newcomer would be a girl because the women were heavily outnumbered by the men in her family, and in her husband's, and she had felt it was time to redress the balance.

'Anyhow,' Sally said, 'boys wear bracelets these days.'

'Not in that family they don't,' said Prudence. 'They're all husky farmers.'

She was part of the family now. The baby's godmother. The Howards had always accepted her and Jean had always been her dearest friend and they were the only family she would ever have.

She went to a Christmas Eve party, and sparkled as brightly as the tinsel, and when she got home she sat downstairs on the sofa with her cat because, although it was late and she was tired, she didn't want to go to bed. She couldn't decide which would be worse— nightmares where she was lost and lonely, or dreams where Jake loved her the way he had that night when everything came right in his arms, but afterwards she would have to wake and know that the dream was over.

When she did finally drag herself to bed her eyelids were heavy, and she slept heavily and woke shivering. She seemed to be in for a chill. She had had that prickling sensation in her nose and eyes yesterday, and slipped out to the chemist's to buy a cold 'cure' that would get her through Christmas Day. She would take a dose before she left home, and she made up carefully, putting on a dark red dress that was warm as well as glamorous.

She could have turned up at the Howards' farm for breakfast and been welcomed, but mid-morning was a more reasonable hour, and at half past ten she put two baskets of gifts on the back seat of her car and headed for Meon Farm. Children were out in the village, rollerskating, riding new bikes and pushing new prams. It was a white Christmas, with sunshine on the snow, and Jean's Christmas baby had come to a loving home.

Nicholas was the star of the day, lying in his crib beside the bed, and Prudence leaned over him and said, 'He's a Howard all right.' Blue eyes looked up at her in a round face, and Jean said, 'Say hello to your godmother, son.'

'Aren't you clever?' said Prudence. She would have liked to pick him up and hug him, but he was very new and he had just been fed. He smelled of warm baby, and she would never have a child of her own because Jake was the only father for them she could imagine, and even if they became friends again, even if the affair rekindled, he would never want that kind of involvement.

Her eyes smarted and she backed from the crib and said, 'I shouldn't be in here, I think I've got a cold coming, but I had to see you both.'

'He's beautiful, isn't he?' said Jean.

'He's perfect,' said Prudence.

Downstairs the festivities went on. Christmas dinner, parcels under the tree. Prudence had a pile of gifts of her own to put in her basket for taking home, and after tea, when dusk fell, she wandered out of the house and walked around the stones on the hilltop. She had eaten too much, she felt sluggish, she needed a little fresh air and exercise and to get away from her friends for a while.

She was very fond of them all, they were so good to her, but she reached the spot where she had stood at the Hallowe'en party, watching the dancers, wishing her wish. She wished for him again. She would always wish for him. She wished, please come and fetch me

away. But this time nothing touched her but a cold
wind, and somebody was calling her name from the
house.

If the wind and weather were suitable on Boxing Day
the more expert members of the hang-gliding club met
on the hill overlooking Stable Cottage and the
Conference Centre. When Prudence got into her car
that night to drive home she was in two minds about
it, half promising, but by the afternoon she had
decided that it might be a cure for her cold in the
head. She would wrap up really warm and take
another dose of her medicine; and she was there,
setting up her glider, with half a dozen other stalwarts.

Of course it was cold, but it was no longer freezing
hard. Most of the snow had melted, the winds were
lively without being dangerous, and altogether they
were expecting some exhilarating sport.

Prudence rode the rise and fall of the winds, soaring
and sweeping, looking down at the familiar terrain
with its unfamiliar patchwork of snow. The next time
she was up here the little house down there would no
longer be her home, she was moving out next month,
and she might as well have taken Jake house-hunting
with her, because he would haunt any home she had.
She would always be dreaming of him, seeing him
there, because he was in her head and her heart. Oh,
she had a heart. If she hadn't it couldn't keep hurting.

He would be away until the New Year, they always
made a big thing of New Year's Day in Scotland, but
when he came back to the Centre she would see him
again, and she would make herself beautiful. He *had*
been attracted to her. She would do everything to
make herself attractive again.

She sneezed so explosively that her head began to
swim. Suppose, one day, he was down there in the

Centre grounds again and she dropped like a stone at his feet, would he run to pick her up? She did not feel too good. It was beautiful up here, but cold 'cures' only masked symptoms and it was stupid to go on like this when she could nurse her cold today, and tomorrow because the shop was not opening till Wednesday.

Even through her thicker-than-usual gear the sharp winds were biting, and she slid the control bar and swung her body, bringing the glider coasting downwards. She fluffed her landing slightly, ending in a small drift of mushy wet snow, and that was positively the last straw. After that she packed up.

'The wind's caught you,' she was told, and when she got back home she saw that her face had developed an unbecoming flush and her eyes were bloodshot. She could hardly see through her eyes. Her head felt packed with pepper, and she couldn't stop sneezing. She got out of her clothes, into the warmest winter nightdress she had and her thickest dressing gown. Then she turned on the electric blanket and sat in front of the stove waiting for the bed to warm up. As an afterthought she took her temperature, because now she seemed to be breaking out into a sweat.

She had the thermometer under her tongue when Jake walked into the room. There had been a knock on the front door which she hadn't answered. She hadn't wanted company and she had thought he was hundreds of miles away. Maybe she was in a fever and dreaming dreams. She blinked rapidly, but he didn't dissolve and Prudence gasped and nearly lost the thermometer, mumbling round it, 'I thought you'd gone away.'

'I came back.'

She felt hideous, and she knew she looked revolting. Percy, who had been sitting on a chair, got off and seemed to be almost welcoming Jake. At any rate when Jake stroked the cat he didn't get scratched. When she lifted a heavy hand to take out the thermometer Jake took it from her, checking the reading and said, 'Dear, oh dear!'

'Is it bad?'

'It isn't good.'

She sneezed again. 'I think I got a chill after the party. It was falling in the snow, I think. I've been trying to weather it with something I got from the chemist's.'

'You're doing a lot of falling in the snow lately.' Jake put the thermometer into a cup on the dresser. 'By the way, I want you to stop the hang-gliding.'

When the helicopters started coming in there would have to be rules and regulations, they might have to move, but Ballinger and Merrick couldn't issue orders like this. 'The club won't like it,' she said.

'It's only you I want to stop.' He sat down, facing her. 'You're the only one I find a distraction. Added to which you don't seem too efficient on the landings.'

He must have been watching her, and this meant he hadn't finished with her and it was almost like it used to be. Prudence wished she was well, looking sexy, because then he might want to make love to her. But she was glad he was smiling and she smiled too and said, 'I am, you know, I'm very good. It's just that you've caught my only two duff landings in years; and oh, I am glad to see you, even if you do have a girl in every port.'

'Not that many. I haven't the time.' His grin miraculously softened his harsh face. 'And certainly none as a cover-up for Tanya.'

'I believe you.'

'I'm glad.'

Prudence got up, a little unsteadily, and went over to the bureau. 'I want to show you something.' She took out the newspaper cutting and brought it to him, and he said, 'You were a pretty child.'

He couldn't have recognised her unless he knew her story. 'You knew my father?'

'Only what you've told me about him.' Which was nothing. And lies. 'But I know what you looked like as a child.'

She stared at him, puzzled, then pointed to the cutting. 'That was my father. He was killed in a car crash in Spain, earlier this month. His name was David Sinclair, I used to be Susan Sinclair, although nobody alive knows that now, I think. He left us, my mother and me, years ago, and we never heard another word from him. He just—vanished. He'd embezzled from all our friends, he'd let everybody down. It killed my mother in the end and it left me pretty short on trust. I've never really risked trusting a man since.' She tried to smile, her lips trembling. 'I suppose I've got what they used to call in Victorian novels "a fatal flaw".'

'And a temperature of over a hundred,' said Jake. 'It's bed for you, baby.'

He picked her up again, as he had at the swimming pool, and again she had a feeling of letting go, because it was all right now. Upstairs she let her dressing gown slip off and slid between the warm sheets, turning her flushed cheek to the cool pillow. He pulled up the sheets, stroked back her hair, and she said, 'It could be catching. I could have a virus. I didn't give you a birthday present. What if I give you the 'flu for Christmas?'

'What are you taking?'

'That.' The bottle was on the dressing table.

'They're not a lot of use,' he said.

'It got me through Christmas Day. I went to Meon Farm and stood by the Stones.'

He smiled down at her and she wanted him to stroke her hair again. 'If I'd known that I'd have come for you. I always thought you put a spell on me on Hallowe'en.'

He could always make her smile and she didn't want to go to sleep. She wanted to lie here, warm and have him close to her. 'Do you have to go?' she asked.

'Oh no, I'm staying. Will that chimney take a fire?'

There was a small fireplace up here that was rarely used, but the room was chilly and a fire would be cosy. 'Yes,' she said. 'There's kindling in the kitchen. Do you want a drink? Do you want anything to eat?'

'Just close your eyes.'

If he was staying she could rest. Prudence closed her eyes as a comforting drowsiness crept over her and within a few minutes she was asleep. When she opened her eyes again she thought, for a moment, that she was dozing, because it was dark, although she could see Jake, in a chair by the fire, and she made no sound to break the spell.

The only light came from the fire, but he knew she was awake. 'I'll get you a drink,' he said.

Her throat was sore and hot and when he brought her hot lemon with honey it hurt to swallow at first, then became a little easier as she sat up huddled in her pillows. She thought she might be losing her voice, but when he switched on the overhead light she yelped, 'Please don't turn that on!'

'Does it hurt your eyes?'

'A little, but I must look terrible. I need a dim light, the fire's plenty bright enough.' He switched it off and she said, 'But I don't look anything like I did when I was a small girl. Did you really recognise me, or did you just guess?'

'I recognised you,' He sat on the side of the bed. 'Just as I know how you'll look when you're an old woman. Very beautiful still,' he touched her face, 'a few laughter lines here,' from nose to mouth and edging her eyes, 'and a few silver hairs,' his fingers brushed her temples. 'Beautiful and happy.'

That would be a lovely future. 'You seem to know how I used to look,' she said, 'so maybe you do know how I'll be when I'm old, although I can't imagine how.'

Jake said, 'Because I love you,' and Prudence wanted that to be the truth more than she wanted to live to be old, but she made herself smile and joke,

'That's easy to say.'

'Yes, it is.' He was not smiling. 'I'm surprised it's easy, because I've never said it before,' and suddenly she knew he was telling her the truth, and that he always would.

'You mean it,' she said. He took the almost empty cup from her, brushed her lank hair back from her face and kissed her with such tenderness that she started to cry. All the bitterness had gone, all the holding back, she could love and trust him without fear. She was cradled against him, feeling dizzy and feverish, but safe and at peace for the first time for as long as she could remember.

'I missed you,' she said. 'I've been missing you all the time.'

'Thank God for that,' he said, against her hair, 'because I can't keep away from you.'

'Oh, I *wish* I was well!' She wanted him to kiss her and kiss her, but her eyes were swimming and she could only breathe through her mouth. She was in no state to be handled passionately. The spirit was more than willing, but the flesh was fragile.

'You will be,' he said. He lay down beside her and

went on stroking her hair, and she thought, he has the
healing touch. My head isn't aching now, and when my
head's clear and he starts stroking the rest of me all the
aches and pains will melt away. 'Percy didn't scratch
you,' she said.

'Percy and I understand each other. We walk
together at nights.'

'You're having me on!'

'I've met him many a night out there.'

'He never told me.'

'I've watched your windows.' She watched his face,
so close, as he went on, 'It was almost impossible to
explain about Tanya. I told myself if you couldn't
trust me that was the end, but I still knew that you
were the first and the last for me. If there was only
that one night I should still never want another
woman.'

That was how she felt, that there would never be
anyone else. But it had seemed nothing special for
him. She said, 'Next morning you seemed so casual
about it all. As though you'd slept well and got up and
dressed and shaved.'

'I hardly slept at all. I just lay looking at you.'

He was completely, totally hers, and she was his
woman and her place was in his bed, and some time
very soon their lovemaking would set the stars on fire.
'Please come into bed,' she said.

'You should be resting.'

'I'll rest, I'll lie so still.'

She lay still, and his caresses were the gentlest of
lovemaking. In sickness and in health, she thought, for
richer for poorer, and as though he read her thoughts
Jake, said, 'Will you marry me?'

He waited for her answer, not breathing. She knew
he had stopped breathing, although he must know
what she was going to say. In the flickering shadows

from the fire she thought he was the most handsome man she had ever seen, and that he would be handsome for the next fifty years. 'We shall make a lovely old couple,' she said. 'I know how you'll look too.'

'Of course we shall.' His breath was on her lips, his heart was beating against her heart. 'But isn't it splendid that we're young now?'

'Yes,' she said, 'oh yes!'

Her skin was glowing as though she lay under a tropic sun, and he said gently, 'Go to sleep now.' He would be tender with her tonight, gentle and comforting, and tomorrow she would be stronger.

'What did you have in mind for when my temperature goes down?' she said, and as he started to tell her she began to laugh.

Harlequin Photo ~ Calendar ~

Turn Your Favorite Photo into a Calendar.

JULY 1984

SUNDAY | MONDAY | TUESDAY | WEDNESDAY | THURSDAY | FRIDAY | SATURDAY

The Browns

Uniquely yours, this 10x17½″ calendar features your favorite photograph, with any name you wish in attractive lettering at the bottom. A delightfully personal and practical idea!

Send us your favorite color print, black-and-white print, negative, or slide, any size (we'll return it), along with 3 proofs of purchase (coupon below) from a June or July release of Harlequin Romance, Harlequin Presents, Harlequin Superromance, Harlequin American Romance or Harlequin Temptation, plus $5.75 (includes shipping and handling).

- -

Harlequin Photo Calendar Offer
(PROOF OF PURCHASE)

NAME_____
(Please Print)

ADDRESS_____

CITY_____ STATE_____ ZIP_____

NAME ON CALENDAR_____

Mail photo, 3 proofs,   **Harlequin Books**   1-5
plus check or money order   P.O. Box 52020
for $5.75 payable to: Phoenix, AZ 85072

Offer expires December 31, 1984. (Not available in Canada)   CAL-1

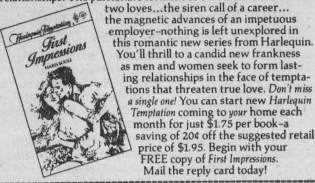